THE DYING OF THE LIGHT

Michael Dibdin was born in 1947, attended schools in Scotland
and Ireland and universities in England and Canada. He spent
four years in Italy where he taught at the University of Perugia,
and he now lives with his wife and daughter in Oxford.
He reviews regularly for the *Independent on Sunday*.

MICHAEL DIBDIN

The Dying of
the Light

faber and faber
LONDON · BOSTON

First published in 1993
by Faber and Faber Limited
3 Queen Square London WC1N 3AU
This open market paperback edition first published in 1994

Printed in England by Clays Ltd, St Ives plc

© Michael Dibdin, 1993

Michael Dibdin is hereby identified as author of this work
in accordance with Section 77 of the Copyright,
Designs and Patents Act 1988.

A CIP record for this book is
available from the British Library

ISBN 0-571-17106-0

2 4 6 8 10 9 7 5 3 1

To the memory of Eileen Coleman

PART ONE

CHAPTER 1

Before entering the lounge, Rosemary paused to check her appearance in the mirror at the foot of the stairs. It was a proper, old-fashioned, full-length looking-glass in a solid rosewood frame, not like the cheap rubbish they turned out these days. That sort of thing might be just about adequate for checking whether your hair was presentable and your seams were straight, but was worse than useless when it came to showing how you looked at a glance, whole and entire.

And that was what mattered, Rosemary reflected, surveying the results of her scrutiny with a certain modest satisfaction. Details were important, of course, but she had been brought up to believe that people were more than the sum of their parts. Anyone with enough money could acquire the trimmings, but what really counted was whether you were the right sort. There was no buying *that*. It was something which registered instantly, without your even being aware of it.

Everyone had their allotted role in the play of life, and the fitting thing to do was to try and look your part. Miss Rosemary Travis was pleased to see that she had been eminently successful in this respect. From her tightly waved silver-grey hair and steady hazel eyes to her sensible tweed skirt and stout rubber-soled shoes she proclaimed herself for what she was, an elderly maiden aunt whose life had been outwardly uneventful but who was no fool, and did not easily suffer those who were.

She opened the door into the lounge. The marble clock on the mantelpiece read ten past four. Tea had not yet been served, but the other guests had already gathered. Colonel Weatherby was installed in his usual chair by the fireplace, reading *The Times*. Some distance away the wealthy invalid Mrs Hiram Hargreaves III, swathed in pullovers and blankets, was whiling away the time with a game of patience. At a table near the French windows giving on to the lawn, Charles Symes and Grace Lebon were bent over a jigsaw puzzle, their heads almost touching. His back pointedly turned to the beauties of the landscape, Samuel Rosenstein stood muttering into the telephone in a guttural undertone. Lady Belinda Scott sat rigidly upright on the piano stool, her fingers lightly touching the keys, while in the corner Canon Purvey nodded over a book. Only George Channing, the corned beef millionaire, appeared to be missing.

Rosemary made her way towards the bay window where her friend Dorothy Davenport sat absorbed in her knitting.

'I've got it, Dot!' she announced excitedly.

'I do hope it isn't catching, dear.'

'No, I mean I've worked out who did it.'

The clacking of Dorothy's needles ceased as she turned her pale, elfin face to Rosemary.

'Did what?'

'Why, the murder, of course!'

4

Dorothy looked away and completed a few more stitches.

'Which murder?' she murmured. 'There have been so many.'

'Well, only two *recently*,' Rosemary replied. 'And of those it's Hilary Bryant's death which has really mystified us, because it seemed that none of the guests could have killed her – although of course one of them must have.'

Dorothy Davenport gave her friend a weak smile.

'I'm sorry I keep forgetting. I think it must be my medicine.'

'I'm just as bad,' Rosemary said quickly. 'Half the time I can't even remember which day it is.'

Dorothy laid down her knitting.

'Oh, I know *that*. It's the day Dr Morel is to call with the results of my tests.'

She winced suddenly. Rosemary bent forward and touched her hand.

'Is it painful?'

Dorothy shook her head.

'It's not that.'

'What, then?'

Dorothy looked at her friend.

'I'm frightened, Rose.'

Rosemary frowned.

'But there's no earthly need to be frightened,' she declared in a peeved tone. 'I told you, Dot, I've solved the mystery. I know who the murderer is.'

Dorothy did not seem to hear. She gazed past Rosemary at the window, where the light was starting to fade.

'They'll send me to hospital,' she said. 'I know they

will. And once they've got me there, they'll keep me, with tubes and wires stuck in me, like an animal in a laboratory. I won't even be able to die, Rose. What kind of life is that, when you aren't able to die?'

'Nonsense!' cried Rosemary scornfully.

Dorothy clasped her hand.

'And you won't be there to say "Nonsense!". That's what I mind most of all, Rose. That you won't be there.'

Rosemary looked away, disconcerted by the intensity of terror in her friend's voice. Then, with a visible effort, she turned back.

'Pull yourself together, Dot!' she snapped. 'There's simply no time for this sort of silliness. We've got work to do. There's a killer on the loose, and he – or she – may strike again at any moment.'

Dorothy's gaze gradually lost its intensity. She relaxed her grip on Rosemary's hand and took up her knitting again.

'Remind me where we'd got to,' she said.

Rosemary released a long sigh.

'Like Roland Ayres, Hilary was found dead in her bed one morning,' she went on. 'Dr Morel seemed satisfied that she had died of natural causes, and in due course signed a death certificate to that effect, but we knew better.'

Dorothy nodded.

'The rat poison kept in the potting shed . . . '

' . . . accessible through the kitchen garden . . . '

' . . . where all the guests went at one time or another in the days preceding Hilary's death . . . '

' . . . under a variety of more or less flimsy pretexts ranging from replacing a missing croquet hoop to questioning the gardener about his begonias.'

Dorothy picked up her knitting again and began to count her stitches.

'And of course they all had a motive,' she muttered.

'Of course!'

Rosemary gestured towards Belinda Scott, who sat gracefully fingering the keys of the piano.

'Revenge! The only man Lady Belinda ever loved was Randolph Fitzpayne, the dashing youngest son of the Earl of Devon. Hilary Bryant dallied with his affections, then broke off the engagement. In despair, Randolph became a sheep farmer in Patagonia, where he was killed in a duel by a drunken gaucho. Lady Belinda never forgave the faithless temptress who had blighted both their lives.'

She pointed to the military man poring over his newspaper.

'As for Weatherby, he was the chief beneficiary of Hilary Bryant's will, which the colonel's flattering attentions had ill-advisedly induced the former beauty to change in his favour just a few weeks before her death . . . '

Rosemary's finger swung across the room to settle on the blanket-enshrouded form of Mrs Hiram Hargreaves III.

' . . . all unbeknownst to the dead woman's sister, who was under the illusion that *she* would inherit in the event of her sibling's untimely death.'

Dorothy smiled happily.

'Yes, it's all coming back to me. But what about Purvey? Surely a man of religion must be above suspicion?'

Rosemary shook her head.

'As one of the guests, he is by definition a potential

suspect. Besides, if you remember, we decided that Purvey is in fact no clergyman but the penniless actor whom Hilary married in her youth, only to abandon him when she met Randolph Fitzpayne.'

'While Grace Lebon is his present wife and accomplice, as yet unaware that their marriage is a hollow sham . . . '

' . . . and Charles Symes the raffish society burglar who is pretending to make love to her – a mutual deception which suits both their purposes – while plotting to steal the priceless but ill-fated diamond known as The Evening Star which Randolph Fitzpayne gave Hilary Bryant in a vain attempt to bind that faithless heart to his.'

Dorothy plied her needles energetically.

'In short,' she said, 'they *all* had a motive to poison her.'

'All except George Channing, the corned beef millionaire,' agreed Rosemary. 'Unfortunately they all had an alibi, too.'

'Even Rosenstein?'

Dorothy pointed to the Jew, who was still muttering urgent phrases into the phone.

'He seemed the most likely suspect for some time,' Rosemary admitted. 'Samuel Rosenstein had every reason to wish Hilary Bryant dead, since she was blackmailing him over the matter of his shady share-dealings. Moreover it was he who passed her the poisoned glass of wine at dinner that evening . . . '

' . . . and then knocked over his own glass, staining Grace Lebon's dress red in an eerie presage of the horrors to come . . . '

' . . . except that it wasn't his own but the *poisoned*

8

drink,' Rosemary continued, 'which he was forced to spill deliberately in order to avoid having to drink it himself when Hilary, suspecting his murderous intent, cunningly switched their glasses. Yes, Samuel Rosenstein certainly planned Hilary's death, but he did not in fact kill her.'

Dorothy gazed eagerly at her friend.

'Then who did?' she breathed.

The door swung violently open and a thickset woman wearing stained blue overalls came rushing into the lounge.

'Where the fuck's Channing?' she bellowed.

No one moved, no one spoke. The woman stood panting in the centre of the room. Her skin was blotchy and uneven, her hair grizzled. Her eyes took in each of the residents in turn: the colonel with his paper, the elderly hypochondriac swathed in blankets, the gay couple by the window, the financier holding the telephone, the languid aristocrat at the piano, the mild-mannered clergyman reading in the corner.

Weatherby waved his folded newspaper.

'I say,' he called, 'is our tea at all imminent, do you happen to know?'

The woman strode over and struck him resoundingly across the face. She wheeled round on the others, her slim red tongue licking the tips of the fingers which had delivered the blow.

'The *first* thing I'll do to our George is make him tell me how he got out,' she said meditatively. 'If it turns out that any of you had a part in it, the only tea you'll get'll be Channing's piss, hot from the kidney.'

She jerked her arm up, making Weatherby flinch, and scuttled rapidly out.

9

The door wheezed shut on its pneumatic spring. After a moment the click of Dorothy's needles resumed.

'Then who did?'

Rosemary gave her a startled glance.

'Who did what?'

Her voice was low and tremulous. Dorothy gave her a searching look.

'For heaven's sake, Rose, I thought *I* was getting bad! Have you already forgotten what we were talking about? If Samuel Rosenstein didn't kill Hilary Bryant, who did?'

Rosemary breathed deeply in and then out. She flashed a smile at Dorothy.

'George Channing.'

Her friend was clearly taken aback.

'The corned beef millionaire? But we've agreed that he was the only person who had no possible motive.'

Rosemary nodded.

'Not as George Channing, no. *But George Channing never existed.*'

Dorothy gasped. Rosemary leaned forward confidentially.

'The man we know as Channing is none other than Randolph Fitzpayne, who went to Argentina to bury his sorrows after Hilary Bryant broke their engagement and his heart!'

Dorothy completed a row of stitches while she thought it over. There was now only a short length of yarn left dangling.

'But Randolph was killed by a drunken groucho,' she objected.

'Gaucho,' murmured Rosemary. 'Yes, so we all assumed. But we have only Lady Belinda's word for that, don't forget. The truth is that Fitzpayne survived the attack and went on to make his fortune in the corned beef trade before returning to wreak his vengeance on the woman who had spurned him three decades earlier.'

Dorothy smiled blissfully.

'And now he's fled to evade capture,' she said, as the free end of the wool inched its way over her knuckles. 'It all fits together!'

She contemplated the panel of knitting for a moment before sliding it off the needle and starting to unravel it.

'Why hasn't Lady Belinda gone with him, though?' she remarked. 'After all, they must have been in it together.'

'She'll join him later, once the hunt for George Channing has been called off. Then they can settle down in the villa he's purchased in Antibes and savour the happiness denied them for so long.'

Dorothy rapidly unpicked the knitting she had been working on. Small knots in several places showed where the yarn had previously been broken.

'Until the police come to arrest them, of course,' she said. 'After all, they can't be allowed to get away with it, can they?'

Rosemary shook her head gravely.

'That would never do, Dot.'

Another spasm passed across Dorothy's face.

'I'll just pop upstairs and fetch my medicine,' she said.

Rosemary looked at her with an expression of concern.

'Is it bad?'

Dorothy shook her head.

'It's just there. It's always there.'

'Let me go,' Rosemary offered.

Dorothy waved her away.

'I need to go to the lav anyway, and you can't very well do *that* for me!'

Rosemary watched her frail, diminutive figure recede across the lounge, passing each of the other residents in turn. By the empty fireplace, Weatherby sat slumped over the newspaper whose pages were yellow and brittle with age. Mrs Hargreaves lay on the sofa turning over a pack of battered postcards showing views of Bognor, Hove and Bournemouth, the written messages so blurred that they were no longer decipherable. The elderly couple were still poring over the jigsaw cannibalized from the surving pieces of what had originally been several separate puzzles.

'Operator, get me the police!' urged the gaunt figure in an intense whisper, seemingly oblivious of the fact that the lead dangling down from the phone ended in a frayed mass of severed wires. Studiously ignoring everyone else, Belinda Scott sat draped over the piano whose strings and mechanism had long been removed. As Dorothy reached the door, Purvey looked up from the pages of his engagement diary for 1951 and smiled at her. 'Thank you once again so very much for letting me impose on your hospitality like this,' he said. 'I do hope I'm not being too much of a nuisance.'

Rosemary glanced at the clock, which still read ten past four. She turned towards the window, attracted by a sound outside. Owing to the plastic sheeting which had been taped over the glass to improve the insulation and reduce draughts, it was impossible to see anything outside and the lounge was never aired. On hot days, and in winter when the storage heaters were turned on, the residual stench of flesh and food and urine, always pervasive, became quite overpowering. She could still hear the noise which had drawn her attention in the first place. Then she had thought it might be a fly trapped between the glass and the plastic film, but now it sounded more like a distant growling interspersed with cries which might almost have been human.

Rosemary got up and raised the lower right-hand corner of the plastic, where the tape had come loose from the frame. Through the triangle of grimy glass she could see part of the overgrown lawn at the front of the house and the double row of copper beeches which marked the line of the driveway, but there was no clue as to the cause of the strange sounds, which had now ceased.

A hand grabbed her wrist, forcing her to release the plastic sheet.

'I'm telling!'

Belinda Scott stood glaring indignantly at Rosemary. Pinned to the bosom of her dress she wore a tattered red paper poppy which she had retrieved from the rubbish bin where it had been discarded by Miss Davis. She pointed to the loose flap of plastic.

'I've caught you red-handed vandalizing official property!'

'Calm down, Belinda,' said Rosemary.

'Don't you dare tell me to calm down, you old bag! I'm telling Miss Davis! They'll stop your meals! They'll give you jabs!'

'No, please, I didn't mean it!' cried Weatherby suddenly, as though in the midst of a dream.

13

Grace Lebon stood up, knocking her chair over.

'I don't like it here,' she announced. 'I want to go home.'

'Well tough titty, 'cos you can't!' retorted Belinda, turning her wrath on this new target. 'They don't want you at home. Not that we want you here either, but we're bleeding stuck with you, aren't we? So if this place isn't good enough for your royal highness, why don't you do us all a favour and just *die?*'

'MY BUM!' shrieked Charles Symes. 'JESUS GOD ALMIGHTY, MY BUM!'

'No, no, please!' moaned Weatherby, swaying to and fro. 'Please don't!'

Belinda Scott strode purposefully about the room, singing at the top of her voice.

'But it really doesn't matter if I'm always slightly pissed, 'cos you'd none of you be missed! Y-o-u'd n-o-n-e o-f y-o-u b-e m-i-i-i-i-i-i-i-i-i-i-i-i-i-i-i-ssed!'

Purvey wrung his hands and looked on imploringly.

'I wonder if I could possibly impose on your hospitality for just one more night?' he pleaded to no one in particular. 'Don't turn me out, I beg of you. I'd gladly leave at once, only I have nowhere else to go, you see.'

'I demand to speak to the police immediately!' hissed Samuel Rosenstein frantically into the disconnected telephone. 'Our lives are all in danger!'

'GOOD JESUS CHRIST, MY BUM!'

'I don't like this hotel! I want to go home!'

'N-o-n-e o-f y-o-u b-e m-i-i-i-i-i-i-i-i-i-i-i . . . '

Rosemary was about to put her hands over her ears to shut out the deafening tumult when the door opened and all the residents immediately fell silent. When they saw it was only Dorothy Davenport, one or two started up again half-heartedly, but they broke off when they saw the expression on Dorothy's face.

'What is it?' cried Rosemary, hurrying over to her friend. 'What's happened, Dot?'

Dorothy stopped just inside the door, pale and trembling.

'I . . . I saw . . .'

Rosemary took her arm.

'What? What is it?'

Dorothy burst into tears.

'Oh Rose,' she sobbed, 'there was blood everywhere! His clothes ripped to shreds and great gashes all over his face and hands!'

She shivered.

'God knows what they can have done to him, poor man.'

'To whom?' asked Rosemary.

Dorothy looked at her friend dully.

'George Channing,' she said. 'The corned beef millionaire.'

CHAPTER 2

'And what do you make of this interesting development?'

The two friends were sitting side by side in their usual places. Dorothy's hands and lips were still quivering and her eyes sightlessly scanned the opaque screen of the window. The other residents, exhausted by their recent outbursts, had resumed their stupor.

'I suppose it was something we should really have foreseen,' Rosemary went on. 'Nothing is more usual, after all, than for the principal suspect to become the next victim. Indeed, my reluctance to consider such an eventuality was perhaps at least partly due to a feeling that the device had become rather hackneyed.'

Dorothy gave a convulsive sob. She reached out and took her friend's hand.

'He's dead, Rose.'

'They're all dead,' Rosemary returned briskly. 'We shouldn't have any victims otherwise.'

Dorothy shook her head violently.

'This is different, Rose. This is serious. They really killed him!'

Rosemary raised her eyebrows.

' "They", Dot? Do you think there's more than one person involved, then?'

'You know who I mean! They were carrying him in when I crossed the hallway. There was blood everywhere, his face was scarcely recognizable. It looked as though he'd been ripped apart by some . . . '

Rosemary withdrew her hand with a genteel shudder.

'There's no need to descend to vulgar melodrama, Dorothy, even if . . . '

She broke off abruptly.

'Oh Dot!' she laughed. 'You are clever!'

Dorothy stared at her blankly.

'You completely took me in!' Rosemary went on admiringly. 'It's the classic technique, disguising the essential clue in a passage of gory sensationalism, and I almost fell for it. "His face was scarcely recognizable." Of course! *That*'s the solution!'

Picking up the shapeless mass of frayed yarn which Dorothy had unravelled, she started to wind it rapidly into a neat ball.

'We've established that Randolph Fitzpayne assumed the identity of George Channing in order to do away with Hilary Bryant. Now that has been achieved, he needs to cover his tracks so that he and Lady Belinda Scott can elope to their villa in Amalfi . . . '

'Antibes.'

Rosemary nodded and smiled.

'Beg pardon, Dot, you're quite right. In Antibes. And how better to ensure that his crime is not brought home to him than by killing off George Channing? The police can't arrest a dead man – especially one who never existed in the first place!'

She handed the completed ball of wool to her friend.

'But if it wasn't Channing I saw, then who was it?' Dorothy protested feebly. 'There isn't anyone else.'

'There isn't anyone else to be the murderer either,' Rosemary pointed out.

'What about Mr Anderson and Miss Davis? I saw them carrying the body upstairs between them, like a sack of coal!'

Rosemary gave her a withering look.

'Well, of course! That's what staff are for, isn't it? Fetching and carrying and suchlike tasks may safely be entrusted to them, but never murder. That's an absolutely fundamental principle. Otherwise what possible interest could the solution have, for heaven's sake? Being killed by a servant is a fate of no more interest than being run over by a tram. No, no, the murderer must be someone like us, someone who *matters*.'

Dorothy threaded the wool on to her needles again and began to form the first stitches.

'Yes, but there isn't anyone else,' she repeated. 'Don't you remember? We were all gathered here in the lounge.'

'All except you,' murmured Rosemary.

Dorothy's hands became still.

'What do you mean?'

'I am merely pointing out that you are the only one who doesn't have an alibi,' Rosemary replied. 'You left the lounge under the pretext of going to powder your nose shortly before the attack occurred, and returned immediately afterwards to stage an extremely convincing display of hysteria.'

Dorothy laughed and resumed her knitting.

'Oh rubbish! What possible motive could I have?'

'One can always invent a motive,' Rosemary sniffed.

'You might be the sultry Latin temptress with whose affections Channing, alias Randolph Fitzpayne, trifled in the course of his sojourn in Patagonia and who subsequently followed him to England intent on exacting revenge.'

Dorothy glared at her.

'Honestly, Rose! Do I look like a dago?'

The door was opened by a lanky man in his mid-forties wearing a blue blazer and white flannel trousers. His long florid face rose to a mat of slicked hair which had receded to the centre of his skull. Holding the door ajar, he wheeled in a metal trolley supporting a large teapot and a pile of cups and saucers.

'Good afternoon, campers!' he called jovially.

There was a scattered muttering of 'Good afternoon, Mr Anderson.'

The man picked up a cut-glass tumbler from the trolley and took a leisurely gulp of the amber liquid it contained.

'And how are we this afternoon, Mavis?' he asked Mrs Hargreaves, who beamed back.

'Don't you worry about me, Mr A! This old heart will see me out.'

'I dare say it will, Mavis. I dare say it will. Although not I trust before you've taken the opportunity to attend to the little matter we discussed the other day.'

He gave Mrs Hargreaves a broad wink.

'I'm giving it a piece of my mind, Mr A,' she replied.

'While the rest of that picturesque organ pursues the more abstruse ramifications of unified field theory, no doubt.'

Mrs Hargreaves gave him an arch look.

'Rome wasn't built yesterday,' she said.

Anderson took another gulp of his drink.

'True. I would none the less draw your attention to the equally well-attested facts that man – or, in your case, woman – does not live by bread alone, and that there is no time like the present. Incidentally it may interest you to know that another of our number has recently taken the pledge, I mean plunge. Unfortunately I'm not at liberty to reveal her name, or indeed sex . . .'

Mrs Hargreaves giggled.

'Beg pardon?'

' "Sex", Mavis. What people have in at least one sense and occasionally two, although not for some considerable time in my case and yours too I should imagine, but don't get any ideas. As I was saying, the benefactor asked to remain anonymous for reasons which I am of course bound to respect, although I confess myself unable to fathom them.'

He drained his glass.

'No, on second thoughts, fuck it. It was Mrs Davenport.'

Rosemary was unable to stifle a gasp. Anderson walked over and placed his hand on Dorothy's head.

'We're all one big happy family here, so I can't see any need to make a big secret of the fact that dear Dorothy asked to see a man of law last week with regard to changing her sex, I mean will. The details naturally remain *sub rosa* not to mention *in petto*, but I can reveal that Letty had to go and round up a couple of villagers to act as witnesses since she and I were ineligible. Make of that what you will!'

Leaving Rosemary staring in shock at her friend, Anderson wandered back to Mrs Hargreaves. He picked up one of the postcards laid out in rows on the blankets.

'We really should see about getting you a proper pack of cards, Mavis. No reason why you shouldn't be playing with a full deck in one sense at least, eh?'

He swept his arm around in an inclusive gesture.

'I don't suppose a television would go amiss either, to say nothing of a more varied diet. My sister's cooking can hardly be described as anything more than adequate at best, but I seem to remember that you had Irish stew and tapioca pudding ten days in a row recently, which probably constitutes some sort of human rights violation.'

He sighed deeply and shook his head.

'Given the necessary funds, there's really no limit to what one might do in the way of superior amenities and improved living conditions. But although Mrs Davenport is to be congratulated on doing the decent thing in leaving her money to benefit our little community rather than the hordes of ungrateful relatives who can't even be bothered to send her the odd wish-you-were-here from Torbay never mind come to visit, I was unfortunately unable to persuade her to come across here and now, up-front, in real time. Result, we can't cash in till she stiffs out.'

He shook his head sadly.

'How ironic that the decease of our benefactor and dearly beloved companion should thus become, to some extent at least, a consummation devoutly to be wished! How much more fitting, how infinitely more desirable all round, if the cash were to be made available in the form of a long-term, unsecured, interest-free loan, no strings attached, no questions asked!'

He swung round on Mrs Hargreaves, arms outspread in dramatic appeal.

'What do you say, Mavis? Yes or no? What's it to be? Give us your answer, do!'

Mrs Hargreaves simpered.

'I believe in burning my boats when I come to them, Mr A.'

Anderson sighed deeply.

'Very well.'

He looked around, taking them in one by one.

'But I must warn you – *all* of you – that unless someone comes across with a sizeable injection of the ready in the very near future, then you will all be facing privation on a hitherto unimaginable scale. There is simply no telling what measures I may be obliged to resort to in my desperate attempts to make ends meet. Certainly this latest tragedy could have been avoided if we'd been able to retain the services of extra staff.'

He pointed at Dorothy.

'I take it you've told them about Channing?'

'Blood!' cried Belinda Scott. 'She said there was blood everywhere!'

Anderson nodded brightly.

'There *was* a certain amount in evidence, I must admit. In point of fact the togs I was wearing at the time got fairly comprehensively besmirched – hence the present nifty outfit with its subtle overtones of naphthalene.'

He upended the glass and let the final drop roll into his open mouth.

'Fortunately the damage seems to be considerably less serious than we first feared,' he went on. 'Letty applied first aid immediately, and with any luck the effects will hardly be noticeable once the garments in question have been to the cleaners.'

He sighed deeply.

'Channing, on the other hand, resembles the proverbial dog's dinner – as is only to be expected under the circumstances. We're expecting Dr Morel any moment with the results of Mrs Davenport's tests. He should be able to give George a shot to put him out of his misery.'

He shook his head sadly.

'Never try and outrun a Dobermann. It awakens their atavistic instinct to mutilate prey.'

There was the sound of a car drawing up outside.

'Ah, I expect that'll be Jim now,' Anderson remarked.

He gave Dorothy a sympathetic smile.

'You'll naturally be anxious to learn your fate as soon as possible, Mrs Davenport. Is the cancer rampaging through your body like a forest fire out of control, sweeping all before it, or is it at present confined to a specific organ or member which might conveniently be gouged out or lopped off? That's the question we're all asking ourselves, and I'll let you know the answer just as soon as Jim's patched up old Channers. Meanwhile do help yourselves to tea. For your own sake, I would strongly advise you to try and avoid making too much mess. Judging by what I found floating in the loo this morning it's Letitia's time of the month, and you know how touchy she can get, particularly after a stressful day like this. Bye-eee!'

With a cheery salute, Anderson walked out. One by one, the residents got up from their chairs and formed a silent huddle around the tea trolley, where Belinda Scott took possession of the pot.

'Right!' she barked. 'From the front, in alphabetical order! Ayres?'

There was an awkward silence.

'Isn't he dead?' muttered Grace Lebon eventually.

'Miss Scott to you!' rapped Belinda.

Leaving Dorothy slumped in her chair, her head tilted to one side as though to hear better, Rosemary walked over to the trolley.

'Roland and Hilary are both dead,' she said. 'Mr Channing is confined to his room, so Dorothy is next. As she's feeling poorly, I'll take it to her.'

'No you won't!' snapped Belinda Scott. 'You'll bloody well wait your turn like everyone else.'

She started to fill the thick, chipped cups with tea, adding a splash of milk to each and placing a sachet of sugar in the saucer. When her own turn finally came, Rosemary took a cup for herself and one for Dorothy and walked back to where her friend sat staring down at the faded floral design of the red linoleum.

Rosemary broke open the paper sachets and poured the contents into the grey liquid, its surface filmy with whorls of grease.

'This would be a good way to kill someone,' she murmured.

The silence was broken only by the clink of crockery and the sound of Mr Purvey sucking tea through his dentures.

'How many is it now?' Dorothy asked suddenly.

Rosemary gave her a cautious glance.

'How many what?'

'And no one ever investigates, do they?' Dorothy went on. 'After all, it's the most natural thing in the world for old people to die.'

25

Rosemary sipped her tea.

'It's not a question of common or garden death,' she remarked dismissively. 'It's a question of *murder*.'

Dorothy gave a wan smile.

'Oh well, that's different, of course.'

Rosemary picked up one of the empty sachets.

'All the killer would need to do is steam one of these open carefully, so as not to tear the paper. Then he . . .'

She paused, eyeing her friend expectantly.

'Or she,' Dorothy murmured at length.

Rosemary nodded.

' . . . would refill the sachet with poison . . .'

' . . . from the potting shed in the kitchen garden . . .'

' . . . where everyone has been at some time or another . . .'

' . . . on some more or less feeble pretext,' concluded Dorothy. 'Yes, but how would you make sure that the intended victim was given the poisoned sachet?'

Rosemary frowned.

'I hadn't thought of that.'

Dorothy sipped her tea.

'Cocoa would be better,' she said.

'But that's already sugared,' objected Rosemary.

Dorothy's needles clacked assiduously.

'Yes, but it tastes so strong that you could add poison without the victim noticing.'

Rosemary shook her head.

'You've still got the same problem, Dot. The mugs of cocoa are just left out on a tray in the hall. There's no way of making sure that the poison reaches the right person.'

Dorothy set down her knitting. She cradled the tea cup in her hands, as though to warm them.

'I always take the blue one. Most people use the same mug every night. Yours is the brown one with the broken handle glued back on. Charles likes the dark green one, while Grace prefers the pale pink. Weatherby always uses that hideous coronation mug, and Mrs Hargreaves . . . '

'You haven't really changed your will, have you Dot?' Rosemary interrupted.

Dorothy picked up her knitting without answering. Rosemary looked at her friend with a preoccupied expression.

'It's none of my business, of course,' she went on, 'but I must say that I would personally consider it most unwise to put any faith in promises which may have been made in a certain quarter. I shouldn't think there's the slightest chance of their being honoured.'

Dorothy clutched her chest and moaned.

'What is it?' cried Rosemary in alarm.

'I'm all right. Only would you be an angel and fetch my medicine? What with one thing and another I never did manage to get upstairs, and now it's started to hurt quite badly.'

'Is there anything else?' asked Rosemary, springing to her feet.

Dorothy tried a smile which did not quite come off.

'Could you possibly spare that thick cardie of yours? I feel the cold so now that winter's here.'

'Of course you can. Although it's only September, you know. Or October at the latest.'

'Does it matter?' Dorothy returned in an oddly muted

voice. 'You can't change anything with words, Rose. I'm *cold*.'

CHAPTER 3

Rosemary made her way along the corridor which wound about the first floor of the building, connecting the various bedrooms. Most of the doors were either closed or slightly ajar, but at length a further bend in the passage revealed one which lay wide open. The room inside looked as though it had been prepared for a guest who had not yet arrived. The furniture was the same as in all the other bedrooms: a sturdy metal-framed single bed with a cabinet beside it, a chest of drawers, a large wardrobe and a hard armchair.

Everything was in its place, corners aligned and not a speck of dust to be seen. The bed was perfectly made, the corners of the covers turned down as though in readiness for the intended occupant. On top of the chest of drawers the various paraphernalia which Mr Purvey needed to keep his diabetes under control were arranged in a precise geometric pattern. Although he had been a resident for several years, Purvey still acted as though he were an uninvited guest who had long outstayed his welcome. Perhaps because of this, he kept his room irreproachably clean and tidy and always left the door open, to indicate that he was not claiming any rights of privacy, still less possession.

Rosemary opened the door opposite and went inside.

She always appreciated her fortune in having one of the smaller bedrooms, which had escaped subdivision. As a result, the walls were solid and the proportions made sense, with two good-sized windows overlooking the grounds at the front of the house. Despite the thick patina of grime on the glass, there was a fine view over the flat expanse of the former croquet lawn, the rockery beyond, and then the pastures rising to the ridge which overlooked the valley. There was a minor road somewhere up there, and when the intervening hedgerows and trees were bare one could sometimes catch a flash of colour as a vehicle sped by.

The noise of footsteps drew her attention abruptly back to the foreground, where a figure in a dark overcoat was striding across the weed-spattered gravel to the blue saloon car parked outside the house, clicking and creaking intermittently as its engine cooled. The man opened the rear door and reached inside. Rosemary hastily stepped back into the shadows of the room as he turned round again, holding a black medical bag. Then the footsteps crunched back to the house again, and the front door distantly slammed.

Rosemary pulled open the middle drawer of the chest which stood between the two windows and lifted out a green cardigan, exposing a panel of sallow newsprint with an article about an agricultural fair. She pushed the drawer closed, overcoming its slight tendency to jam, and was about to open the door when she heard the noise of rubber-soled shoes in the corridor outside.

'Ahm alwuss trahin',' sang a powerful female voice. 'Fower to make dat punishment fit dat crime! Sure am! Lordy! Bet your sweet ass!'

Rosemary waited until the squelching footsteps had

receded before venturing out. Closing the door carefully behind her, she hurried off along the corridor towards Dorothy's room. This was situated on the north-facing side of the building, which meant it got no sun and had a much less attractive view over the former kitchen garden, stables and other outbuildings. To make matters worse, the original room had been divided to accommodate extra guests, back in the far-off days when Eventide Lodge had been a flourishing enterprise under the energetic direction of old Mrs Anderson.

Since her son had taken over, death had steadily reduced the number of residents, but the partitions remained in place, strips of flimsy plasterboard through which you could hear everything that happened in the neighbouring room. This was particularly unfortunate in Dorothy's case since her neighbour, George Channing, snored loudly. Rosemary had tried to have her friend transferred to Mr Purvey's room, next door to her own, but Mr Anderson had told her that 'to avoid any suspicion of favouritism' residents must retain the room they had been allocated on arrival.

The doorway to the two adjoining rooms gave into a cramped plasterboard cubicle from which plywood fire-retardant doors led off on either side. Rosemary was about to open the door into Dorothy's room when she heard a loud groan from behind the walling to her right. After a moment's hesitation she grasped the handle of the other door, stepped inside and stood open-mouthed and staring, struck dumb by the sight which met her eyes.

The room was in chaos. Blood-stained clothes lay strewn about. There was more blood on the walls, as well as on the overturned chest of drawers and the broken chair. The floor was littered with shards of glass. A cold draught swept in through the smashed window, making the curtains flap wildly. But Rosemary barely noticed any of this. All she could see was the body outstretched on the bed, roped to the frame at wrist and ankle, covered in gashes and abrasions, the skin deathly pale, the torn clothing blotched with blood.

The man's mouth was bound with sticking tape, but his eyes were fixed on Rosemary's with manic intensity, and his whole body seemed to resonate with the eerie moaning. But before Rosemary could think what to do, let alone do it, she heard voices nearing along the corridor outside. With a helpless glance at the man she hurried out, closing the door quietly behind her, and slipped into Dorothy's room just before the two speakers reached the doorway.

'Shame he didn't break his damned neck while he was at it,' Anderson was saying. 'Injured's no good to me, Jim. I need them dead.'

'You want the police called in?' replied a man Rosemary recognized as Dr Morel. 'They die in bed is one thing, but I can't just rubber-stamp something like that. Should have put bars on the windows.'

'It all costs money, you know. Besides, it doesn't look good.'

'And how good do you think this looks? An ex-Battle of Britain ace trying a stunt like this at eighty something. People are going to wonder why he bothered.'

'No they aren't, Jim. Because they aren't going to find out, as long as you keep your mouth shut.'

'And then to set the dog on him . . .'

The voices became muffled as the two men entered

the next room and closed the door behind them. Rosemary walked slowly over to the window, hugging the green cardigan to her chest. The walled kitchen garden below was now overgrown with brambles whose long tendrils had matted together to form an impenetrable mass of spiny undergrowth. A narrow path of concrete slabs had been kept open, leading from the back door to a doorway in the wall. Halfway along it was a rough clearing where Anderson's Dobermann was normally kept tethered. Now its orange nylon cord lay limp on the ground amid the dog's massive droppings.

The murmur of voices was still audible next door, although only the occasional word was intelligible from where Rosemary was standing. She tiptoed over to the bed, crouched up on it and put her ear to the wall.

'Jesus Christ almighty!' Morel exclaimed. 'Do you file that hound's teeth or what?'

'Klaus is an attack dog,' replied Anderson haughtily. 'His jaws are the result of generations of selective breeding.'

'Pity they forgot to leave room for a brain.'

'It was his own fault, Jim. If Klaus hadn't got him, he'd probably have been hedgehogged by some passing motorist.'

'All I'm trying to say is you can't run a place like this by yourself, Bill.'

'Letty's not just a pretty face, you know.'

'I mean someone human. And preferably with a few relevant qualifications.'

'It all comes down to money,' Anderson sighed. 'Speaking of which, what's the good word *in re* the Davenport?'

Rosemary jerked her head away abruptly from the

wall. She got down off the bed and crossed to the chest of drawers on the other side of the room, where Dorothy's meagre stock of personal possessions were displayed. There was a small statue of a lighthouse inscribed 'Land's End', a faded photograph of two solemn children holding hands, a set of miniature spirit bottles in a wooden case, a Chinese fan with a broken gilt clasp and a spray of dried poppies. There was also a brown bottle with a typed label reading *The Mixture Mrs D. Davenport To be taken as directed Do not exceed the stated dose*. A transparent plastic spoon was attached to the bottle by a rubber band, its bowl lightly stained with a blue smear.

Taking the bottle in one hand and holding the cardigan under her arm, Rosemary walked quietly to the door. In the cubicle leading to the corridor the voices once more loomed up at her.

' . . . out of the question,' Morel was saying. 'I've read the consultant's report, Bill. The only way she's going to leave hospital is in a bag.'

'Fine, but *when*?'

'That's hard to say. Could be a few months, could be a year. Someone our age you'd be talking weeks, but the old last longer, funnily enough. The metabolism's running down, you see, so even a rampant malignancy like this takes a while to run its course.'

'So what if she tells the nurses about our chum here? If this gets in the papers . . . '

'Don't fret, Bill. She'll be out of it on pain control most of the time, plus with the staffing levels these days no one has the time to stand around nattering.'

'All the same, I'd be happier if she stayed here.'

34

'No can do, Bill. Once the machinery's been set in motion . . . '

Rosemary ran as fast as she dared along the corridor to the landing and clattered downstairs. Catching a glimpse of herself in the mirror, she noticed that she was patting the back of her right hand, which held the medicine bottle. That gesture had been the closest her mother, an undemonstrative woman, had ever come to physical intimacy, and then only on very special occasions when she had felt it necessary or desirable to reassure the child – in much the same way that she kept a small bottle of brandy on the top shelf of the cupboard in the bathroom 'for medicinal purposes only'.

Rosemary turned briskly away. That was quite enough of that. She wasn't having mirrors going soft on her. Shiny, hard and shallow was how she wanted them, reflecting her as she was, as she appeared to be, an elderly maiden aunt whose emotions were under perfect control at all times. It was a relief to return to the lounge and find the other guests all in their places: the colonel with his newspaper, the peeress at the piano, the clergyman buried in his book, the lovebirds using the jigsaw as an excuse for their proximity, the invalid widow swathed in her blankets, the Jew on the phone. Only George Channing, the corned beef millionaire, appeared to be missing.

Rosemary slipped into the chair beside her friend.

'We must talk, Dot!' she said urgently. 'Here, put the cardigan on. I've been a fool, Dot. No, not that button, there's one right here at the bottom. We've been totally and utterly wrong all along, and I almost didn't realize the truth until it was too late! Quick, take your medicine and then I'll explain.'

She held out the brown bottle to Dorothy, who shook her head.

'It's eased again.'

'Are you sure?'

'I'll keep it until I really need it. What were you saying about being wrong?'

Rosemary leant forward and regarded Dorothy earnestly.

'Our fundamental mistake all along has been to assume that there was a logical motive for each of the murders which have taken place so far,' she said. 'We've taken it for granted that Roland Ayres and Hilary Bryant were killed for revenge, or for their money, or to silence them. Now a third member of our little group, George Channing, has become the target of a seemingly senseless act of . . . '

Dorothy twisted impatiently in her chair.

'Why is Dr Morel taking so long, Rose?' she broke out. 'Don't they know how hard this is for me? Why can't they just tell me and have done?'

'Pull yourself together, Dorothy Davenport!' snapped Rosemary. 'We're facing a ruthless and cunning killer who has already struck three times, and while I don't yet know who he – or she – may be, I *do* know the identity of his – or her – next victim.'

Dorothy smiled wanly.

'Can you save him, Rose?'

'Her.'

'Who?'

'You.'

Dorothy's eyes widened.

'Me?'

'I'm so sorry,' Rosemary sighed. 'Try and be brave.'

'But . . .'

'It came to me in a flash while I was upstairs. I was thinking of what happened when we had tea. Do you remember? Belinda Scott was annoyed because of something that happened when you were outside the room, so she insisted on serving the tea in strict alphabetical order . . .'

'But you had to wait until the end, even though you were getting my tea too. I didn't think that was fair, Rose. You shouldn't have stood for it! If I'd been you, I'd have . . .'

'That isn't the point!' hissed Rosemary. 'The names of the victims so far are Ayres, Bryant and Channing. Now do you understand? The killer is eliminating the residents in alphabetical order. *Which means that you will be the next victim!*'

Dorothy tut-tutted.

'Come on, Rose!' she exclaimed with a toss of the head. 'This simply won't do. It sounds like one of those awful American books about some maniac who goes about chopping up total strangers with an axe because he had an unhappy childhood. Not my cup of tea at all, I'm afraid. Life is quite horrible enough as it is, I should have thought, without scaring oneself silly with such rubbish.'

Rosemary smiled in a superior way.

'That's precisely what the killer wants us to believe. The plan – and I'm bound to say it's a very clever one – is to create the impression that these killings are indeed the work of some distasteful psychopath such as you describe, whereas in reality all *except one* are simply red herrings designed to obscure the identity of the murderer's true target.'

Dorothy's eyes narrowed. She gave her friend a suspicious look.

'Wait a minute,' she said. 'This has been used before, hasn't it?'

'Are you accusing me of plagiarism?' snapped Rosemary.

'Of course not, Rose. It's just that, well, it has a familiar ring to it.'

'This is no time to discuss the finer points of the genre, Dot! Every minute you remain here you are in the most terrible danger. This very night might be your last! We must get you out of here at all costs.'

'Don't be silly! No one's ever managed that. Look what happened to Channing.'

Rosemary clasped her friend's hand and smiled confidently.

'We'll think of a way.'

Dorothy shook her head.

'Anyway, why should anyone want to kill me? It doesn't make sense. I don't like it when things don't make sense, Rose. And I don't want to go. I want to stay here with you. I'm sure you must be mistaken about this. After all, we're the detectives. The detectives never come to any harm, do they?'

The door banged open and the woman in the stained blue overalls swept into the lounge again. She looked round the room with a contemptuous sniff and then made for the corner where Rosemary and Dorothy sat talking. When she reached the centre of the room, however, she stopped and sniffed the air again, more deliberately this time. Then she turned round slowly, inspecting the residents, each of whom looked away as the beam of scrutiny passed. Eventually it came to rest on the pair still bent over their jigsaw puzzle. The woman hitched up the straps of her overalls. A feral grin convulsed her features.

'Symes!'

Charles Symes quivered slightly but did not look up. The woman walked slowly towards him, swaying her hips in a slow sinuous rhythm.

'To let the punishment fit the crime,' she crooned softly.

She stood over Charles Symes and Grace Lebon, sniffing loudly. With a violent movement of one hand she swept the completed section of the jigsaw off the edge of the table. It broke up and fell to the floor in pieces.

'Look at me, Symes!' she howled.

Slowly, painfully, the man turned his head.

'My nostrils suggest that you've beshat yourself,' the woman remarked conversationally.

Charles Symes stared up at her without moving.

'Do they deceive me?' she inquired.

There was no sound in the room. The woman bent closer.

'Well, Symes?' she demanded in a stage whisper. 'Which of us is at fault, my nose or your bum?'

She straightened up abruptly.

'On your feet and let's have a gander.'

A high-pitched keening made itself heard in the room. Swivelling on her heels, the woman slapped Grace Lebon hard with the back of her hand. The sound abruptly ceased. The woman sniffed her fingers briefly, then crooked one at Symes.

'Make yourself erect, man!'

Symes rose from his chair, his face a mask.

'Drop 'em!' commanded his tormentor.

With trembling fingers, Charles Symes struggled to undo the buttons of his trousers. The last one wouldn't come free of the hole. After watching him fiddle with it in vain for some time, the woman reached across and tore the fastening loose. The trousers fell heavily to the man's ankles, revealing the wrinkled, sheeny expanse of his buttocks smeared with a brown glutinous mess.

'Oh my Christ!' the woman exclaimed.

She gazed at the spectacle in disgust for some time, wiping her hands on the front of her overalls.

'What I ought to do,' she remarked at length, 'is make you lick it up and then cauterize your arse with a red-hot poker. But seeing as my hands are full with Channing I'll settle for a cold shower and Dettol rub followed by a night locked naked in the outside loo to remind you what that facility is for. Now fuck off out of here before I puke, you filthy old bastard.'

Holding his trousers loosely round his hips, Symes hobbled towards the door. The woman turned expressionlessly to the others. She walked over to Belinda Scott and plucked the paper poppy from her dress.

'Remembrance Day's long past, Lindy. Not that you have anyone to remember, do you? Or anyone to remember you.'

She tore the flower apart, petal by petal, and let the pieces fall to the floor.

'*Do you?*' she insisted.

'No, Miss Davis. Sorry, Miss Davis.'

The woman nodded.

'Still, look on the bright side, eh? At least you might still be in the land of the living come next Poppy Day, unlike some people I could mention.'

She shot out a finger at Dorothy, who got to her feet. Rosemary also stood up. Miss Davis raised her eyebrows at her.

'No one rang for you, Travis.'

Rosemary squeezed her friend's hand.

'I'll wait for you here, Dot. Don't worry, it'll be all right.'

Miss Davis sauntered over to them. She leaned very close to Dorothy, searching her face.

'Yes, it'll be all right,' she said. 'Just as long as you keep your trap shut, don't fidget, shoulders back, tummy in and knickers clean. Otherwise you know what'll happen, don't you?'

Miss Davis stared at her intensely, her face a couple of inches from Dorothy's. She leaned forward suddenly and kissed her on the mouth. Dorothy gave a muffled cry. When Miss Davis drew back, there was blood on her lips.

'Yes, you know,' she said. 'You've dreamed about it, more than once. Only this won't be a dream, my poppet. This will be real.'

She snatched Dorothy's hand and led her to the door while Rosemary looked on in helpless anguish.

CHAPTER 4

As dusk gathered beyond the plastic-shrouded windows, the light in the lounge imperceptibly faded, until the residents were no more than insubstantial shapes merging into the outlines of the furniture. For the most part they were silent, but from time to time one would suddenly burst into speech. This set others off, until soon the whole group was yattering inconsequentially away, all talking, none listening. Then as suddenly as it had begun it would stop, each speaker breaking off in mid-sentence until the final voice ceased and silence resumed once more.

This time it was Samuel Rosenstein who started it. His name was actually Rossiter, but Rosemary and Dorothy had needed a Jew to complete their cast of suspects.

'Hello? Hello?' he shouted into the telephone. 'Operator? Connect me to the police immediately!'

Next Jack Weatherby chipped in with a few stray phrases from the news bulletins he had once read on the BBC World Service.

' . . . on the clear understanding that the respect of such demagogues can only be won by a show of force, thus enabling any eventual negotiations to proceed from a position of . . . '

43

' . . . turned my back for a single instant,' cried Grace Lebon, whose real name was Higginbottom or something equally unthinkable, 'to look at something which had caught my eye in a shop window, and when I looked round again the pram was empty!'

' . . . can't say when I've enjoyed myself so much,' broke out Purvey, a retired accountant who had no more connection with the Church than Weatherby with the Army. 'Unfortunately the last train seems to have gone, so if it wouldn't inconvenience you too terribly I wonder if . . . '

This brought Belinda Scott to her feet.

'We've got to take under our wings, tra-la!' she bawled at the top of her voice. *'These perfectly loathsome old things, tra-la!'*

As the tumult rose about her, Rosemary gave a panicky glance at the clock, which of course still stood at ten past four. How long had Dorothy been gone? Rosemary had said she would wait for her, but how long would that be? Would she return at all? They might already have dragged her off to hospital, trussed and gagged on a stretcher like Channing on his bed.

As the realization of what her friend's absence was going to mean came home to Rosemary for the first time, she felt her control begin to slip away. For years now they had been at each other's side night and day. It was always Rosemary who had taken the initiative. It was she who introduced new twists and turns in the story which they had elaborated together, she who kept all the strands of the plot in play while still managing to accommodate – and thus to some extent control – the real horrors which surrounded them.

In contrast, Dorothy's had been the subordinate role.

Her task had been to fill in the gaps which Rosemary left blank for her, to spot the errors which Rosemary had deliberately planted for just that reason, to approve and criticize, suggest and reject. Thus when Rosemary had allowed herself to consider the possibility of Dorothy being sent away to hospital, she had seen it in terms of her friend being cut off from *her*, and hence from the source of the comforting narrative which had sustained them both for so long. Now she was forced to acknowledge that her own position would be little better, in that respect at least.

The stories were a collaboration, she realized now, and although Rosemary had always been the dominant partner she could no more keep them going by herself than one player, however brilliant, could have a game of tennis with no one on the other side of the net. A sense of panic gripped her at the thought of her coming isolation, of the fear and uncertainty and loneliness she was going to have to endure, night and day, without respite or relief. She would end like the others, just another voice in that chorus of manic despair.

She felt someone touch her arm and looked round to find Mrs Hargreaves gazing down at her with an expression of concern. Hargreaves was in fact the woman's real name, although Rosemary had tacked on the 'Hiram' and 'III' to make her sound more like a rich American widow. By now she had grown so accustomed to thinking of Mrs Hargreaves as a petulant, cold, selfish hypochondriac that she was initially shocked rather than comforted to hear her say kindly, 'You look just about at the end of your feathers, Miss Travis.'

45

'I'm fine!' Rosemary rapped back in a manner which challenged the woman to deny it.

'You're sure there's nothing I can do you for?'

'I can manage perfectly well on my own, thank you,' Rosemary shouted, only to find that the tumult of competing voices had died away. To make amends for her rather aggressive tone, she added, 'I felt a bit giddy for a moment, but it's passed.'

'I'll just come and sit with you until she gets back,' said the woman, taking Dorothy's place.

'There's no call for that, Mrs Hargreaves. I'll be quite all right now.'

'Call me Mavis.'

Rosemary, who had no intention of ever calling anyone Mavis if such a thing could possibly be avoided, smiled remotely.

'Terribly kind of you, I'm sure, but . . . '

'Two hands are better than one, I always say.'

Rosemary's smile became still more distant.

'You and Mrs D,' ventured the other woman cautiously, 'you're very . . . very *close*, aren't you?'

Sitting in Dorothy's chair, Mrs Hargreaves had her back to the window. In the gathering darkness, it was impossible to make out the expression on her face.

'We're friends,' said Rosemary.

'Oh I didn't mean there was anything, well, you know . . . '

Rosemary kept silent.

'Not that I'd mind one way or the other,' Mrs Hargreaves went on breezily. 'I used to be quite partial to a touch myself at one time.'

Rosemary decided it was time to regain the initiative.

'I gather that Mr Anderson is endeavouring to persuade you to alienate your estate in his favour, Mrs Hargreaves.'

'Mavis.'

There was a silence.

'Mavis,' Rosemary conceded.

'Now then, what was that about Mr A?'

'I just said that it sounds as if he's trying to get his hands on your money,' said Rosemary.

Mavis Hargreaves giggled.

'Well, you know men.'

'I shouldn't take anything for granted.'

'Oh I didn't mean *you*, dear! I wouldn't dream of . . . '

'Anything Mr Anderson may say, I mean,' Rosemary explained stiffly.

'Don't you worry about that! I wouldn't trust our Mr A as far as I could kick him out of bed.'

'After all, Hilary Bryant made her money over to him shortly before she died, and much good we saw of it.'

Mavis Hargreaves nodded.

'Keep them chasing the carrot at the end of the rainbow, that's what I always say.'

She placed a plump white finger on Rosemary's knee, which instantly twitched aside.

'It's your friend you should be worried about, by the sound of it.'

Rosemary bit her lip.

'I'm sure there's no truth in that.'

'Mr A seems to think there is.'

'What does it matter what he thinks?' demanded Rosemary shortly.

There was a creak of hinges at the far end of the room, then Dorothy's voice.

'Rose?'

She was on her feet in a moment.

'Coming, Dot!'

The room was in almost complete darkness by now. Rosemary made her way slowly towards the door, her one thought to help her friend face up to the terrible news which had just been broken to her, and very likely in the most casually brutal fashion. She must get Dorothy out of there, she thought, away from the inquisitive Mrs Hargreaves and all the others, up to her room, where she could go to pieces without making a spectacle of herself.

'I can't find the light switch,' Dorothy called faintly from somewhere near by.

'Never mind, I'm nearly there.'

A few moments later they were in each other's arms, and Rosemary had guided her friend to the sofa beside the door. They sat in silence for some time, holding hands.

'I know, Dot,' Rosemary said at last.

'The news, you mean?'

Dorothy's face was just a blur, but her voice sounded strangely calm. Rosemary nodded, then realized that she was invisible too.

'Yes,' she said. 'When I was upstairs, I overheard Dr Morel talking to . . . '

She sat there in silence, despising herself for her selfish weakness in breaking down at the very moment when her friend was more than ever in need of her strength and support.

'I don't know what to say, Dot,' she added lamely, when she could trust herself to speak.

'I know,' Dorothy murmured. 'It's like a miracle.'

48

As a child, Rosemary had an uncle whom her mother pronounced 'common', just about the worst failing in her book. Murdering someone didn't necessarily lower you socially, but the said uncle's tendency to bark 'Eh?' when he failed to hear, understand or approve of a statement made to him she regarded as an unforgivable lapse of taste. The young Rosemary's attempts to imitate this shameful trait had been ruthlessly repressed, but she could not now prevent herself emitting the vulgar vowel, such was her astonishment.

'Just think!' Dorothy went on. 'There you were telling me how vital it was for me to get away from here before I became the next victim. And now, as if by magic, that's what's going to happen! Miss Davis took me to Mr Anderson's office. Dr Morel was there. He told me that the tests I had showed that I needed to go into hospital straight away . . . '

She broke off. Rosemary squeezed her hand. Dorothy gave a little laugh.

'So there we are! Isn't it wonderful?'

Rosemary finally understood, among many other mysteries, why Dorothy had pretended to be unable to locate the light switch. She too was grateful for the darkness, which reduced all the intolerable complexities of what they were suffering to a mere exchange of dialogue characteristic of the parts which they had elected to play. She had created these parts herself in an attempt to make a fictional virtue of the factual necessity for Dorothy to return to hospital. The idea of the alphabet murderer had been a feeble contrivance, stolen – as Dorothy had not scrupled to point out – from a half-remembered whodunnit, but it was the best she had been able to do in the time at her disposal, still numb

49

with the shock of what she had overheard Morel and Anderson saying.

Dorothy, for her part, had evidently decided to accept it in the spirit in which it had been offered. She did not really believe that her life was in imminent danger, of course, but was pretending to do so in order to spare both of them the pain and confusion that would otherwise be unleashed. It was a supremely civilized piece of behaviour. Neither was taken in by the other's act, but each would play her role to the end.

'Wonderful,' echoed Rosemary.

But Dorothy had not exhausted her capacity to surprise.

'For me, yes. But what about you, Rose?'

'What about me?'

Dorothy withdrew her hand.

'Oh, I know what you must be thinking!' she exclaimed. ' "It's all very well for Dot, but what about the rest of us?" And it's true, Rose. *I'll* be safe enough, but you will still be here, in his . . . '

She laughed.

' . . . or her power.'

The breeziness of her tone quite disconcerted Rosemary. For a moment she felt a shiver of apprehension, as though something uncanny was afoot, something she had not planned and did not understand. It was quite in order that Dorothy should wish to appear calm and collected. What was disturbing was that at moments Rosemary had a distinct sense that she really *was*. Ever since learning that she might have to go to hospital, Dorothy had been on the verge of a tearful collapse at the mere idea, yet now the worst had occurred she seemed immune, floating above it all, as though it were a matter of no personal concern to her at all.

'His or whose power?' she murmured vaguely.

Dorothy gave a snort of impatience.

'The murderer's, of course!'

The door swung open and all the lights came on.

'Murderer?' cried Mr Anderson. 'What murderer?'

He stood over the two women, nosing his tumbler of whisky. As Rosemary's eyes adjusted to the glare, she made out Miss Davis circling round from the other side. She was holding a tall stemmed glass filled with layers of different-coloured liquids – tawny, green, red, blue and yellow – topped by a miniature umbrella.

'You'll get fucking murdered, if you don't watch out,' she said.

Ignoring her, Rosemary looked at Anderson.

'We were discussing a book.'

'A book?' Anderson replied.

He raised his eyebrows and then frowned, sipping his drink.

'I dimly recall that among the amenities available to residents under the former regime was a selection of trashy whodunnits and mawkish romances such as might be expected to appeal to persons of low taste and declining faculties, but they've long since gone the way of everything else round here that isn't nailed down. Might I therefore ask to which book you allude, Miss Travis?'

Rosemary waved airily.

'Oh, one Dorothy read years ago, during a wet weekend in Wales. She was just describing the plot to me.'

Miss Davis lifted the paper umbrella from her drink.

Her lips englobed the maraschino cherry impaled on the stick below.

'Liar,' she said.

'Now, now,' murmured Anderson. 'Don't let's spoil the party.'

He took a gulp of whisky.

'Nevertheless,' he continued, 'given that Mrs Davenport cannot always be relied upon to recall with any accuracy what she had for breakfast, it does at first sight seem hard to believe that she should be waxing lyrical, still less logical, about some shilling shocker she once read in Rhyl.'

'Pwllheli,' Dorothy put in.

'Bless you, dear!' murmured Rosemary.

Miss Davis sucked at the upper layer of her cocktail.

'Lying bitch,' she said.

Anderson fixed Rosemary and Dorothy with a penetrating stare.

'I put it to you, ladies, that so far from discussing a whodunnit, you were in fact concocting one.'

'Well?' said Rosemary. 'And what of it?'

Anderson glanced at Miss Davis.

'Did you hear that, Letty?'

'I did, William. I did indeed.'

'Miss Travis wishes to know what of it.'

'Impertinent cunt. Do you want me to take steps?'

'Not at present, I think. After all, we must make due allowance for the situation in which the two ladies find themselves. Parting is such sweet sorrow, and so on. *Partir, c'est mourir un peu* – or, in Mrs Davenport's case, a lot. Let us therefore endeavour to rise above petty considerations and address her question.'

He turned back to Rosemary and Dorothy.

'I realize that time can hang pretty heavy round here, especially so, paradoxically enough, for those with very little left. Nor has it escaped my attention that your favourite way of passing it has been to work up elaborate scenarios of imaginary mayhem featuring those who have left us feet first as the victims, the dwindling band of survivors as the suspects, and your good selves as the intrepid sleuths. Hitherto I have had no particular reason to take exception to this, but the case is now altered. If an outsider were to witness an exchange such as the one which Letty and I just overheard, the resulting disruption to the life of our little community would be quite intolerable. I must therefore ask you, Mrs Davenport, to put these tall tales of dark deeds at Eventide Lodge very firmly out of your mind.'

He turned to the other residents.

'I should explain that from tomorrow dear Dorothy will be with us no more. Despite my objections, to say nothing of her own stated preferences, the powers that be have decreed that she is to be transferred to hospital, there to undergo a course of treatment which according to Dr Morel is not only hideously painful and degrading but completely pointless when the carcinomata are, in his memorable phrase, "sprouting like fungi on a dead tree".'

'Stop!' cried Rosemary, getting to her feet. 'I won't have you talking like that! I won't stand for it!'

With a howl of fury, Miss Davis flung her glass at Rosemary. It shattered against the wall a few inches away. Miss Davis advanced, screaming obscenities, her spittle flying into Rosemary's face.

'Easy, Letty!' warned Anderson, grasping her arm.

'Let's leave Mrs Davenport with fond memories of the old place, eh?'

Miss Davis's body went limp. She breathed in and out deeply several times.

'Of course, William,' she said eventually. 'Whatever you say.'

Ignoring Rosemary and Dorothy, she flounced out of the room, singing merrily.

'And that's why I mean what I say when I sing, O bugger the flowers that bloom in the spring. Tra-la-lala-la-ha! Tra-la-lala-la-haaaaaaa!!!!! Bugger the flowers of spring!'

Anderson inspected the rainbow of liqueurs splashed across the wall.

'Drambuie, Green Chartreuse, Cherry Brandy, Blue Curaçao, Advocaat,' he murmured, shaking his head sadly. 'Poor Letitia! She suffers so greatly.'

He glanced pointedly at Rosemary.

'One more outburst like that from you, Miss Travis, and you'll be spending the rest of the week in bed with Mr Channing.'

He drained the rest of the whisky from his glass.

'Life is one thing, ladies, and art quite another. Far from being a story which alternately excites and consoles, life is an endless slurry of computer print-out, a pie chart of statistical trends in which you, I fear, have been allotted the slimmest of slices. Always remember, however, that even that might be taken from you.'

Favouring them both with a smile, he walked out.

CHAPTER 5

The light outside seemed to have faded completely, yet when the fluorescent ceiling strip suddenly died the darkness turned out to be hollow. There was still an afterglow of radiance, too faint to compete with the synthetic glare but enough, once their eyes had widened to take it in, for Rosemary and Dorothy to make out, if not everything, then quite as much as they had any real need or wish to see.

'That's better,' murmured Dorothy.

The bed springs squeaked as she snuggled down.

'Much,' Rosemary replied from her chair by the window.

Each was aware of the other as a vague, benevolent presence in the dimness, barely visible but very definitely there. The electricity on the first floor was switched off at nine thirty every night, except when Anderson and his sister were too drunk to remember, but this abrupt transition had never felt so welcome before.

Dorothy's room was ugly enough in itself, its proportions mutilated by the partition, the original features badly dilapidated and the new ones scruffily utilitarian, but tonight its charmlessness was intensified almost unbearably by their shared, unspoken knowledge that it would never again be Dorothy's room. This was the last time they would sit there in the darkness, adding yet more strands and complications to the murderous web of intrigue they had woven around themselves. Next day the room would be locked, like those of the residents who had died.

Under the pitiless glare of the neon light these facts had been impossible to evade or ignore, but the darkness arrived as a balm, waiving the imperatives of space and time. In that dimensionless obscurity there was only here and now, an endless present and everything within reach.

'Aren't you going to drink your cocoa?' Rosemary suggested gently.

'Not yet.'

'It'll get cold.'

'It already is. All those people. Still, it was nice, wasn't it?'

Rosemary said nothing. The phrase seemed so far from the mark, so grossly inadequate to the situation, that she might have suspected Dorothy of irony if she hadn't known that her friend was literal-minded to a fault. Whatever else it might have been, the incident certainly hadn't been *nice*. It had been bizarre, embarrassing, unpleasant, sad, and finally rather moving. But Rosemary's most vivid impression, both at the time and now, was of utter astonishment that it had ever taken place.

The scale of the transgression involved had been made clear when Miss Davis burst into the room, having been tipped off by Belinda Scott. By that time they were all there. Mavis Hargreaves had been the first to arrive, having 'just popped in on the way back from the loo'. While she was standing there at rather a loss, wondering what to say next or how best to leave, there was a timid knock at the door, followed by Weatherby's voice asking if Dorothy were 'presentable'. Grace Lebon and Charles Symes appeared next, accompanied by Alfred Purvey, and it was at this point that Belinda Scott put her head round the door, gasped, and promptly disappeared. Rossiter, who arrived shortly afterwards, reported having met her running along the corridor calling for Miss Davis.

This news might have been expected to break whatever spell had descended on the residents that evening, but – much to their mutual surprise – it did not. Not only did they all stay, but on the face of it they seemed less flustered by the risks they were running than by the embarrassment of bidding Dorothy goodbye. It thus initially came as something of a relief when the door flew open and Miss Davis stormed in, with Belinda Scott at her heels.

'Right, back to your rooms!' she barked at them. 'No fraternization permitted! Contrary to fire regulations! Break it up, break it up!'

But against all expectations the party refused to be broken up. Perhaps it was their very terror which impelled them to the unprecedented step of defying Miss Davis. The thought of what she might do if she were to get them alone merely increased their determination not to be separated. The outcome was equally startling. Never having had to face a situation like this before, Miss Davis proved to be at a loss as to how to deal with it.

When threats and orders had no effect, she tried hitting one or two of the nearer residents, but was at once disabled by the others. No word was spoken, yet all seemed to understand what they must do. Aged and frail as they were, they could not offer active opposition, but they could and did very effectively get in the way, hampering the younger woman's freedom of action, pushing her off balance, holding her back and hemming her in, until with a cry of mingled rage and panic she broke free and forced her way back to the door.

'Very well, then!' she shouted furiously. 'Go ahead and wish your precious chum goodbye before she's packed off to the abattoir. But just remember this! She'll be strip-searched before she leaves, and if I find any begging letters, billets-doux or other foreign matter concealed in her cracks and crevices, the person responsible will get it for lunch, with the rubber gloves as afters!'

Belinda Scott tried to say something, but Miss Davis slapped her across the face and stalked out, leaving her rejected acolyte to run off in tears. The others remained, the awkwardness which had briefly been dispelled now returning in full force. To Rosemary, the scene appeared increasingly grotesque and disgusting, a hideous caricature of everything hateful about their lives: the cruel light, the sordid room, the men and women variously disabled in mind and body, strangers both to themselves and to each other, reciting their impotent good wishes and empty formulas of farewell.

Then everything changed. Exactly how and when was something Rosemary was not sure of even now. Perhaps it had been when Purvey stumbled against the bedside table, spilling some of the cocoa, and everyone rallied round to help with the clean-up. Or it might have been when Dorothy, her face flushed and her eyes brilliant with tears, thanked them all for coming and urged them to give her friend all the help she would need in the coming days.

Rosemary had found it hard to repress a disdainful scowl at this. Under the circumstances Dorothy could of course say what she liked without fear of contradiction, but she was stretching her privilege to the limit in suggesting that this crew of decrepit geriatrics might conceivably be of any help to Rosemary Travis. She would come to terms with Dorothy's absence in her own way and in her own time. All she asked of the others was that they should leave her alone.

To her dismay, however, the effect of Dorothy's words was exactly the opposite. The other residents all turned to Rosemary as though seeing her for the first time, and smiled or nodded, murmured something, said her name. It wasn't what they did or said that mattered, it was what came with it, a wave of emotion that engulfed them all, filling the room, bringing them together.

Rosemary managed to stand her ground, but she felt cruelly betrayed. She and Dorothy had spent their whole time taking their distance from these people, turning them into cardboard characters whom they manipulated to suit their whims and the twists and turns of the story. Now Dorothy had made them real, given them depth and feeling, turned them into human beings united in this mindless warmth like a litter of animals in a burrow. It wasn't fair, Rosemary reflected bitterly. Dorothy had broken the unwritten rules of their friendship.

She kept her thoughts to herself, of course, even once

the visitors eventually trooped out, leaving them alone together again. Dorothy was putting a brave face on it, but Rosemary knew how she must dread the ordeals and indignities which awaited her at the hospital. If her chosen way of coping was by patronizing Rosemary, that was something she was just going to have to accept in silence. In the event, neither of them spoke until the fire-alarm clattered briefly and, thirty seconds after this warning, all the lights went out. It had been this imposed curfew which had first given rise to the stories. They flourished in the dark, running riot, proliferating wildly, unrestrained by anything but the absolute and eternal rules of the genre.

'Have they told you what time you're leaving?' Rosemary asked.

The figure in bed stirred slightly.

'They don't know themselves.'

Rosemary pondered this for a moment.

'Surely they have to organize transport?'

'It's all taken care of.'

There was a disjointed quality to this exchange which Rosemary found irritating, as though they weren't talking about quite the same thing.

'Well, if and when you find out, perhaps you would be kind enough to let me know,' she replied a trifle waspishly. 'I have my own arrangements to make, you know.'

The darkness secreted something which sounded suspiciously like a laugh.

'You lead such a busy life, Rose.'

Rosemary pointedly said nothing.

'I expect you'll be wanting to get some sleep,' Dorothy added quietly.

At once, the reality of the situation came home to Rosemary with redoubled impact, and she felt dreadfully ashamed of her petulance.

'Do you want me to go?' she asked tremulously.

Again there was a hint of laughter.

'Go? You're not the one who's going, Rose.'

Rosemary felt her irritation flare up once more, but this time she managed to keep it under control.

'Precisely,' she replied. 'I remain here, to try and solve the mystery of these murders as best I can alone.'

'Oh Rose . . .'

Rosemary was glad to note that Dorothy sounded suitably contrite.

'I don't ask for sympathy,' Rosemary went on, 'but any help you might feel able to offer would be most gratefully received.'

There was a brief detonation of bedsprings.

'Do you want me to send in the police?' whispered Dorothy.

Now it was Rosemary's turn to laugh.

'Good heavens no! What earthly use would the police be in a case like this? They would simply go clomping about, obscuring all the clues and falling for every red herring in sight. What I was hoping was that I might continue to be able to count on your own invaluable assistance, Dot.'

There was a long silence.

'How . . . how do you mean?' Dorothy inquired guardedly.

'Well, we might write to each other.'

After a moment, Dorothy laughed again, openly this time.

'I don't know if that will be possible,' she exclaimed.

'It would mean a great deal to me if you could manage even a few lines occasionally, setting out your ideas,' Rosemary went on. 'There's no one here that I can possibly confide in.'

Rosemary congratulated herself on her tone, which contained just the right amount of self-pity to suggest that she was asking Dorothy a favour rather than throwing her a lifeline. She was therefore the more surprised to find the response so grudging and constrained.

'Well, I don't know,' Dorothy repeated. 'I mean, I'll do what I can, of course, but we can't be sure that it's going to be possible for me to remain in touch on any sort of regular basis. All the evidence, indeed, seems to suggest the opposite.'

The residual glimmer from the window had now completely faded. To her dismay, Rosemary found that she was suffering from the delusion that the darkness had started to swirl slowly around the room like a nascent whirlpool. The motion was as yet almost imperceptible, but the sense of what it might become was almost as disturbing as the fact that she could not seem to shake off the idea. If she could have switched on the light, the power of the illusion would instantly have been broken, but that was no longer possible.

'Don't be silly, Dot!' she snapped irritably. 'They're bound to let you send and receive letters. The problem is going to be this end, but I have a few ideas about that which I'll tell you in the morning.'

She rose to her feet.

'I'd better be going. I feel a bit . . . '

She broke off, ashamed of speaking of her own feelings at such a moment.

'I'm so sorry, Dot.'

Dorothy's voice was calm and steady.

'There's nothing whatever to be sorry for.'

She sighed.

'I just wish I could tell you, Rose.'

'Tell me what?'

The winding darkness was drawing her across the room, towards the bed where her friend lay. Dorothy's arms encircled her neck, pulling her down. Their embrace was longer and harder than Rosemary quite cared for, putting a tremendous strain on her detachment and self-control, for she was determined not to blubber.

At last she managed to free herself, and stand up.

'See you in the morning, then!' she said briskly.

As she was about to turn away, her wrist was seized in a grip so intense it was painful.

'The poppies,' she heard Dorothy utter. 'Where do they come from?'

'Poppies?' she echoed lamely.

The fingers clamped about her wrist tightened.

'They used to be everywhere in spring. The fields were full of them. All the soft shades, red and blue and violet. You never see them now, do you? They killed them off with sprays and chemicals . . .'

'You're hurting me!' Rosemary complained.

What she found most disturbing about her friend's incoherent ramblings was that it sounded as though Dorothy thought she was making perfect sense. She was relieved to feel the grip on her wrist slacken.

'Sleep well, Dot,' she murmured soothingly. 'I'll come and wake you in the morning as usual.'

She tried to withdraw her hand, only to find that the tenacious grip was suddenly renewed.

'Yet whenever they break the ground to build a road or a housing estate, there they are again, in their hundreds, as though they'd never ever been away! And at other times you never see them. So where do they come from, Rose? Where do they come from?'

Dorothy's voice was raucous with what might have been either terror or triumph, but which in either case Rosemary felt an urgent need to dispel.

'I really couldn't say, Dot,' she replied deliberately. 'But I have no doubt that there's some perfectly logical explanation. What does it matter, anyway?'

The grip on her wrist abruptly ceased.

'It doesn't matter,' Dorothy replied in a dull voice. 'It doesn't matter in the slightest.'

Rosemary remained standing there awkwardly for some time. Once again, she felt that she had unjustly been put in the wrong.

'Good night, then,' she said, a trifle coolly.

'Goodbye, Rose.'

Rosemary turned and moved cautiously across the room towards the door. As she reached it, she seemed to hear her friend's voice in the darkness behind her, saying what sounded very much like, 'I love you.' But the words were very faint, and it was perfectly feasible for Rosemary to spare them both further embarrassment by pretending not to have heard.

CHAPTER 6

She awoke with a sensation of having just left a room in which some terrible scene was taking place. The door had slammed shut behind her, and the voices raised in fury or fear were now just a fading memory. For an instant she seemed to hold the whole thing clear in her mind: she knew who had done what, to whom, and why. No sooner did she examine it, however, than this seemingly inexorable logic revealed itself to be no more than a string of feeble contrivances, rather like the plots of the detective stories with which she had used to read herself to sleep. But while those stabbings, shootings and poisonings had generated only a pleasing drowsiness, the anonymous voices in her dream had raised a terror which was still real.

The sunlight which had wakened her streamed in through the window, making even the worn rug and stained wallpaper look fresh and gay. Brusquely shaking off the torpor which was the legacy of her shallow, broken sleep, Rosemary got out of bed and went to the handbasin in the corner to douse herself with cold water. She had enough real problems on her plate, heaven knew, without indulging in that sort of nonsense!

The air was still chilly, and her breath flared in the

beams of sunlight as she scrubbed and towelled. She had deliberately not drawn the curtains before going to bed the night before. Dorothy was not by nature an early riser, and it had become their habit for Rosemary to go to her room and rouse her. Never had it been more essential for Rosemary to be at her friend's side than this morning, when Dorothy awoke to the reality of her imminent departure.

Although Rosemary had been heartened by the show of composure which Dorothy had put on the night before, she had no great hopes that the effect would last. It was one thing to be brave in advance, she knew, but quite another to retain that equanimity when the moment of truth finally arrived. Which was where *she* came in, as she always had. As long as Dorothy remained at the Lodge, Rosemary would be with her every instant – and even once they were separated, she would be with her in spirit!

The idea she had thrown out the night before as though it were an inspiration of the moment was in fact something to which Rosemary had devoted a considerable amount of thought. She knew it would prove a huge challenge, but that merely gave her a further incentive to bring it off. Such a challenge was just what she was going to need to see her through the weeks and months ahead. It would distract her attention from the anguish she could do nothing about, and focus it on a problem entirely of her own making and subject to her control.

There would be no time to brood on her own loneliness or indulge in gloomy speculations about what might be happening to Dorothy. Each moment of every day would be dedicated to working out the next episode

of the murderous events at Eventide Lodge, a story so
effortlessly complex, so endlessly fascinating, so flaw-
lessly spellbinding, that reality would pale by compari-
son. Even the ordeals which Dorothy had to endure
would be reduced to the status of a minor irritation, an
annoying distraction when you are trying to read. This
time, at least, the tyranny of the real would not prevail.
Rosemary's alternative account, tight and compelling,
never losing its thread or disappointing the expectations it had created, would triumph in the end. She
would answer for that!

The major problem that had to be overcome was the
practical one of ensuring that the letters got through.
There would be no difficulty at the hospital, of course,
despite what Dorothy had rather oddly claimed the
night before. She would be able to send and receive as
many letters as she liked, at least unless – even to herself, Rosemary avoided the word 'until' – her condition
deteriorated markedly.

Rosemary's position was very different. Although the
residents of Eventide Lodge were in theory free to write
to their friend and relatives, the letters handed over to
Mr Anderson to be posted seemed to fall into a void.
Replies either failed to materialize or, almost more disturbing, made no reference to the concerns expressed in
the outgoing letter.

'Why should your nearest and dearest waste their
precious time scribbling wish-you-were-heres when
they're paying William and I good money to make
damn sure you aren't?' demanded Miss Davis rhetori-
cally, and although some of the residents, including
Rosemary, suspected that their post was being
tampered with, this was impossible to prove. Residents

were forbidden to use the telephone, on the pretext that Mr Purvey had thrown a fit when one of his relatives hung up on him, and personal visits had virtually ceased. 'Out of sight and out of our minds,' Mrs Hargreaves had remarked sadly one day, which had just about seemed to sum it up.

The present situation, however, was quite different. During the long hours of a largely sleepless night, Rosemary had worked out a system which she would agree with Dorothy prior to the latter's departure, and which was designed to make it obvious if their letters were being intercepted. Like all good ideas, it was in essence very simple. Every other day Rosemary would dispatch a letter to Dorothy containing the latest episode of the unfolding mystery, ending with the sort of question which traditionally concluded each chapter in a story of this type. 'Who was the mysterious figure who was seen entering Mr Purvey's room shortly before the body was discovered?', for example, or 'Why did Mrs Hargreaves try and take the wrong mug of cocoa, and what is the connection between this and the fragmentary conversation supposedly overheard by George Channing?'

The whole point of detective stories, of course, was that there always *was* a connection. Even if there wasn't, that was equally significant. It was thus a perfect medium of communication in a situation such as this. All Dorothy need do was send a brief message in reply – a few words on a postcard would suffice – alluding to the developments left hanging. If she felt well enough, she might even assay some suggested solution which Rosemary would then tear to shreds, in the nicest possible way, by return of post. There remained the question of what sanctions to take if it became clear that their letters were not getting through. From what Rosemary had overheard the previous day, she knew Anderson was deeply worried that Dorothy might tell the hospital staff what had happened to Channing. She also knew why. Mrs Anderson, the founder and former owner of the Lodge, had been at considerable pains to reassure the residents – many of whom had become her friends – about what would happen in the event of her death. 'I've left it all to William,' she'd explained, 'but only on condition that all of you continue to be properly looked after for the remainder of your lifetimes.' This stipulation had in fact been the original germ of the murder story. As Rosemary had remarked to Dorothy one day, Mrs Anderson had, with the best intentions in the world, given her son a perfect motive to kill them all.

It was this which gave Rosemary every confidence that, whatever might happen to other letters, those between her and Dorothy would be allowed through. She proposed to offer Anderson an arrangement to their mutual advantage. As long as Dorothy continued to receive Rosemary's letters endorsed with a scathing comment or two on the suggestions Dot had appended to her last (*Surely you would have heard anyone going into Purvey's room, Rose? Mrs Hargreaves presumably didn't know that that mug contained the poisoned cocoa. As for what Channing says he heard, that sounds like a red herring.*) then her lips would remain sealed about conditions at Eventide Lodge. But if there was any unexplained hiatus or delay, Dorothy would ask to speak to the chief consultant in confidence, and the next thing Anderson would know the police would be at the door.

Rosemary was well aware that in making such an

agreement she was sacrificing the interests of the other residents – not to mention her own – to ensure Dorothy's peace of mind. She would have found this impossible to justify to herself, let alone anyone else, she realized as she dressed hurriedly, but the question simply did not arise. There was nothing else she could do. In hospital Dorothy would have the best of medical care, but nothing and no one could replace the complex network of fact and fiction which Rosemary had woven into the intimate fabric of her friend's consciousness. By manipulating those narrative strings like a loving puppeteer, she could influence events even at a distance, curtailing Dorothy's isolation, limiting the inevitable pain and damage, protecting, distracting, consoling. She knew Dorothy better than anyone else in the world, she reflected with justifiable pride as she closed the door to her room and stepped out into the corridor. There was nothing her friend could do or think or feel or suffer that she could not foresee and counter.

The house was perfectly silent and deserted at that early hour. Rosemary stepped lightly along the strip of red linoleum, past doors giving on to bedrooms still in use or given over to dust and spiders. At one point there was a low window with a breathtaking view of the parkland at the front of the Lodge, trees, walls and hedges melting insubstantially into a dense layer of low mist above which the sun rose in a pale blue sky. Rosemary reluctantly turned aside to enter the dark plasterboard cubicle opposite. She hesitated a moment before George Channing's door, then tapped lightly on the other side. There was no answer. She turned the handle quietly and stepped inside.

On this side of the house, cut off from the sun, the

dim light made it seem several hours earlier, but the formless mass of the covers revealed that Dorothy was still in bed. Rosemary breathed a sigh of relief. At the back of her mind all along had been the fear that her friend might have spent a sleepless night pacing the floor in growing panic at the prospect facing her. In that case, she might well have been so distraught by now that any attempts to help would have been in vain. The last thing Rosemary wanted to do was to deprive her friend of a single moment of healing rest. All she planned was to be there when the sleeper awoke, ready to offer succour and support.

The room smelt stuffy and unclean. Rosemary went over to the window and raised the bottom sash to allow the clean morning air to flow in. A low growl raised the hairs on her arms and the nape of her neck. In the wilderness of the abandoned kitchen garden below, the tethered Dobermann sat perched on its haunches, every muscle tensed, staring up at her with an expression of pure malevolence.

She stepped quickly back into the room, out of the beast's view. Then, collecting herself with an effort, she forced herself to look out once more. The dog had its back to the window and its nose to the ground, inspecting the results of its previous activity. Rosemary now realized that this had involved nothing more sinister than 'doing its business', as she described it to herself.

With a discreet sniff of distaste, mingled with scorn for her weakness in allowing herself to be frightened by such a thing, she crossed to the chair she had occupied the night before and sat down to wait for Dorothy to stir. The dog's attention must have been drawn by the noise of the window being opened, she thought, and like all animals it disliked being surprised at such a moment. As for the expression she had read in its eyes, Rosemary reminded herself sharply that malevolence, like its opposite, was an exclusively human attribute.

What revived her fear was not another sound but the silence gathering about her, an intrusive and imposing presence in the room. Then there was the smell as well, which she could no longer pretend was just the stuffiness to be expected in a room where someone has been sleeping. There was another component to it, an acrid whiff of something at once familiar and bizarre, intimate and faintly disgusting, which asserted itself above the ambient odours of decay and neglect.

Rosemary got to her feet, looking about her apprehensively. The first thing she saw was the paper, lying on the floor near the head of the bed. It was an ordinary sheet of writing paper, but when she stooped to pick it up, she was surprised to find her name written in block capitals. She turned the page over and quickly scanned the lines of wavery writing on the other side.

She straightened up slowly, seemingly mesmerized by the patch of wall just above the bed, where the grudging daylight made the wallpaper gleam dully. All around, the massed shadows crowded in at the margins of her vision. It was a very long time before she could bring herself to look directly at that darkness, but when she did it immediately receded, laying bare the figure lying on the rumpled covers, the head tilted sideways across the pillow, the eyes staring sightlessly up at the ceiling, the mouth gaping wide, the puddle of vomit collected on the sheets and in the hollow at the base of the throat.

PART TWO

CHAPTER 7

Not so bad after all in the end, thought Jarvis as he slammed the Fiesta's door and crunched across the gravel towards the house. He hadn't been best pleased when Tomkins had come down with food poisoning, leaving him to handle this chore on his own, but the drive out across the hills, not to mention the pint of bitter he'd found time for on the way, had done wonders to bring him round to the idea. As for Tomkins, serve him damn well right. Nothing like a dose of the bloody flux to cure the lad of his addiction to surf 'n' turf bars for the foreseeable future.

He climbed the short flight of steps leading to the front door and heaved on the bell-pull. Gentry did well for themselves in those days, he thought, eyeing the massive boot-scraper. Coming home of a morning, their hand-tooled leather clogged with the poor sods they'd ridden roughshod over. Still, even for the riff-raff it must have been some compensation to know what the rules were, and that they wouldn't change in their life-time.

Were we really that much better off, when you got right down to it? All depends what you mean by better, doesn't it? What is truth? What's it all about, Alfie? Where are the snows of yesteryear? How much is that doggy in the window? Pass, thought Jarvis, whose secret fantasy was to appear on *Mastermind* ('Your chosen subject: Accrington Stanley's line-up, results and week-by-week league position, 1956–1962').

The door was opened by a lanky man in his mid-forties wearing a blue blazer and white flannel trousers. His long florid face rose to a mat of slicked hair which had receded to the centre of his skull. In his left hand he held a cut-glass tumbler filled with an amber liquid. He peered at Jarvis.

'Not today, thank you,' he said, starting to close the door. 'Nor indeed any other day, for that matter.'

Jarvis flashed a regulation smile.

'Mr Anderson? I believe you're expecting me.'

The man eyed him blearily.

'You may also believe that the earth is flat, for all I know. It doesn't follow that such is in fact the case.'

Jarvis felt his guts clench as though in the first stirrings of indigestion. Just when everything had seemed to be going so well. He unbuttoned the dark blue overcoat he'd got half-price in the sales, revealing an acrylic-rich suit from which he produced his warrant card.

'Detective-Inspector Stanley Jarvis, *sir*. I am calling with regard to Mrs Dorothy Hilda Davenport, née Cooke, deceased.'

The man squinted at the warrant card.

'You don't look anything like the person in this photograph.'

'I was given to understand that you had been informed of and had agreed to this visit,' snarled Jarvis, with whom the quantity of weight gained and hair lost over the past few years was a sore point. 'One of my associates was in telephonic communication with a certain . . . '

He took out his notebook.

' . . . Miss Davis.'

Anderson raised his hands in surrender.

'Ah, the fair Letitia! That explains everything. Say no more, Inspector! I'll come quietly, it's a fair cop, lock me up for my own good, I get these terrible urges, etcetera etcetera.'

He opened the door wide and Jarvis stepped inside. The hall was deep, bare and resonant. A boar's head projected from a trophy hung high on one wall. Next to the door stood an elephant's foot hollowed out to take an assortment of sticks and umbrellas. The air was chill and dank, the light dull.

'This way, Inspector!'

Anderson padded across the flagstones towards a lighted doorway. Hush Puppies squealing underfoot, Jarvis followed. The room they entered was small and windowless and smelt strongly of mould. All four walls were covered in shelving crammed with books of every conceivable size, shape and colour. The furniture consisted of a leather armchair which had seen better days and an antique writing-desk supporting an array of spirit bottles.

Jarvis looked round at the serried spines and titles, most of which were either illegible or incomprehensible. Several were in foreign languages. None seemed to have anything to do with the history or fortunes of Accrington Stanley FC.

'Like books, do you, sir?' he remarked archly.

'How very astute of you, Inspector. One can readily see why you have risen to a position of such eminence.

As you so rightly surmise, bibliomania is indeed one of my principal pleasures, the other being alcoholism.'

He selected one of the bottles from the escritoire and poured a generous quantity into his tumbler.

'I'd be more than happy to offer you a dram,' he told Jarvis heartily, 'but generations of literary coppers saying "Not while I'm on duty, sir" have no doubt made it impossible for you to accept such an offer even if you felt so inclined. Thus are we constrained by fictions.'

Leaning his elbow on the mantelpiece, Anderson fixed his visitor with an expression of polite attention. Jarvis realized it was incumbent on him to say something. He consulted his thoughts. They were empty.

'This is just a routine visit, sir,' he declared.

'That's what they all say, Inspector.'

Jarvis cleared his throat.

'Who all?' he demanded. 'I mean, all who?'

That didn't sound right either.

'Along with refusing a drink because they're on duty,' said Anderson, taking a gulp of his whisky.

We've got a right one here, thought Jarvis. He inhaled deeply and massaged the bridge of his nose. Accrington Stanley 4, Stockport County 0. Gateshead 1, Accrington Stanley 1.

'According to the officers called to the scene last Tuesday,' he said, 'one of the patients here, a Mrs . . . '

He glanced at his notebook again.

' . . . *Miss* Rosemary Travis, made certain allegations regarding the circumstances surrounding Mrs Davenport's death.'

Anderson giggled.

'Glitches,' he said.

Jarvis goggled.

'Witches?'

'Bats,' said Anderson, heaving at his whisky. 'In the belfry. Bugs in the program. If our clients – the preferred term, incidentally – were user-friendly, they wouldn't be.'

Jarvis got out his pen and executed a doodle in his notebook.

'Wouldn't be what?' he murmured.

'*In loco clientis,*' replied Anderson as though the point were obvious. 'If they weren't already loco.'

Catching Jarvis's expression, he put his glass down and made pantomime gestures indicating insanity.

'IF ALL THERE, NOT ALL HERE!'

Jarvis assumed an expression intended to impress on Anderson the manner of man with whom he had to do. Catching sight of himself in the mirror over the mantelpiece, he decided he just looked constipated.

'My officers reported that Miss Travis appeared quite rational.'

Anderson shrugged.

'They were expecting maybe the mad scene from *Lucia di Lammermoor*?'

He drained off the last of the whisky and went to replenish his glass.

'They don't tear their hair or foam at the mouth, my little gerries,' he called above the chink of bottles. 'At some of their other orifices, now and then. But by and large most of them give a pretty fair impression of knowing a hawk from a handsaw, if we are to accept that feat as an adequate criterion of sanity.'

He strolled back to the fireplace and took up his former pose.

79

'Appearances, however, are deceptive,' he went on. 'You and I may be constrained by fictions, Inspector, but this lot are haunted by them. Nothing more natural, of course. For while we are lashed to the mast of actuality, our eyes fixed firmly on the future, their present is hanging by a thread and they've no future at all. It is hardly to be wondered at if they occasionally fall prey to siren voices.'

Jarvis ostentatiously consulted the next page of his notebook. It read:

Bank
Chemist: piles
Cleaners – *still* stained
Plonk for piss-up
RITA????

'According to my officers' report,' he said, 'Miss Travis claimed that Mrs Davenport had been murdered by one of the other patients.'

'*Clients,*' snapped Anderson. 'I have no patients, and no patience with such stuff as this. When dear Mamma passed on to the great rest home in the sky, leaving this sublunary one in my unworthy hands, my first thought was to take the money and run to NW3 or possibly the S of F. Unfortunately she had in her wisdom made it impossible for me to sell up as long as the present occupants keep one foot out of the grave. Thus it is that I am forced to eke out my best years in the company of dribblers and bed-bespatterers.'

Jarvis tapped his pen against the notebook.

'Just answer the question, please, sir.'

'You didn't ask a question, Inspector, you raised one.

If you give me half a chance, it will become clear that I am in fact addressing it.'

He swallowed some more whisky before continuing.

'Whatever the drawbacks to the life I lead out here, I have at least had ample opportunity to acquaint myself with the varieties of senile dementia to which my flock are subject. In the case of Miss Travis this takes the form of an inordinate passion for detective stories.'

'I'm not talking about leisure pursuits,' Jarvis interrupted.

'Nor am I, Inspector. I'm talking about death.'

Jarvis added an elegant curlicue to his doodle.

'Yes,' he said, 'but natural or violent? That's the question.'

'Not to Miss Travis,' Anderson returned. 'Such distinctions are bound to appear specious to those facing the prospect of their own imminent extinction. All the residents of this establishment are shortly destined to become the victims of a ruthless and anonymous killer against whom the combined forces of civilization have so far proved powerless. What more natural than that they should seek to contain their terror by recasting themselves as characters in a nice cosy whodunnit, threatened not by impersonal oblivion but a fallible human murderer, acting in a recognizable manner and for comprehensible motives, whose identity will be revealed in the final chapter?'

Stockport County 0, Accrington Stanley 0, thought Jarvis. Accrington Stanley 3, Tranmere Rovers 1. Under the influence of this homely mantra, the stress gradually seeped out of his system. When he could trust himself to speak in a suitably authoritative tone, he looked back at Anderson.

'I shall need to talk to Miss Travis, sir.'

Anderson raised his glass and stared through it darkly at Jarvis.

'My overriding concern must at all times be the welfare of the little community entrusted to my care,' he murmured. 'Those were my dear Mamma's dying words to me. Well, actually she made a noise resembling a washing machine on a heavy soil cycle, but that's what she was trying to say all right. I should know. Christ knows I'd heard it often enough before.'

'Either here or at headquarters,' Jarvis continued implacably. 'It's all the same to me.'

Anderson poured the rest of the whisky into his mouth. Leaning his head back against the wall, he gargled loudly.

'It's not so much a question of the venue,' he said at length, 'as of upsetting the psychological microclimate which Letitia and I strive to maintain here at Eventide Lodge, and which is so essential to our clients' well-being. In this carefully controlled environment, the fictions I referred to earlier proliferate freely and yet harmlessly. But if an outsider – particularly one girded in the awful panoply of the Law – comes crashing in demanding to know the truth, the whole truth and nothing but the truth or God help you, the effect on the delicate and frankly non-viable life-forms whose habitat is thus rudely disturbed is fearful to contemplate.'

'I'm not intending to conduct a formal interview,' Jarvis protested. 'It's just a question of asking Miss Travis a few questions, that's all.'

Anderson sighed.

'Even so, is there really anything to be gained by harassing a sad old lady who lives in a world of her own, which although it to some extent mimics the one we inhabit has in fact only the most tenuous connection with it?'

Jarvis stuck his chin up. His ears gleamed dangerously.

'If you prefer, sir, I can always apply for a court order.'

Anderson butted the wall with his forehead.

'As you wish!' he cried, making for the door. 'I'll get Letitia to round her up. Do with her what you will, Inspector – Miss Travis, I mean. No one in their right mind would want to do anything mentionable with Letty.'

The door closed behind him. Jarvis expelled a breath which he seemed to have been holding for a very long time. Bradford City 6, Accrington Stanley 4. Accrington Stanley 0, Port Vale 0. Crewe Alexandra 0, Accrington Stanley . . .

A cold panic gripped him. Fourteenth of November 1953, the weather dull, crowd of almost seven thousand. Ian Brydon the scorer, Galbraith substituted at half-time and Accrington must have won because of the announcer's rising intonation, but what was the friggin' score?

He slumped down in the armchair and closed his eyes. Such a thing had never happened before. Come hell or high water, he had always been able to quote any Accrington scoreline on demand. Not that there *was* much demand, once the family moved down south. Jarvis had been six at the time, so it hadn't meant that much to him, but his dad had never got over not being able to go along to Peel Park and watch the lads lose.

The team in the town they moved to was non-league,

but his dad didn't reckon that what they played down south deserved to be called football anyway. Even after ten years, Harry Jarvis's roots remained in Lancashire. As time went by his memories became increasingly vague and unreal, and even his accent gradually lost its native edge. In the end only Accrington Stanley FC remained. Every Saturday afternoon, he and his son would sit themselves down in front of the radio in the parlour and listen to the Division Three results: Barrow 3, Scunthorpe United 1. Grimsby Town 1, Wrexham 1. Mansfield Town 2, Accrington Stanley 3.

Sitting beside the hissing gas-fire with a mug of hot tea listening to that plummy voice reciting the familiar litany of names was the high point of Stanley's week. Although the Accrington result was the only one they were interested in, he loved the build-up through the First Division giants, and the poetic coda of the Scottish clubs with names like the title of a romantic novel – Partick Thistle, Queen of the South. Above all, he liked trying to guess the result from the announcer's intonation: rising for an away win, dropping for a defeat – the more sharply, the greater the goal difference – and stressing both names equally if the match was a draw.

The second highlight of the week occurred when a brown envelope with an Accrington postmark landed on their doormat. It contained a letter from Stan's uncle enclosing a cutting from the local newspaper expanding the bare result into a racy and compelling narrative involving their favourite cast of characters being cautioned or sent off, scoring or giving away goals, making heroes or fools of themselves. Stanley devoured these reports like episodes of a thriller, and the facts and figures around which they were built impressed themselves so effortlessly on his memory that he had no idea what a fund of them he possessed until that fateful day in March 1962 when Accrington Stanley made the national news for the first and last time as their sixty-eight-year league existence came to an abrupt and ignominious end.

After years spent bumping comfortably along the lower reaches of Division Three North, in the mid-Fifties the club suddenly rose to finish within the top three for several years in succession. Harry Jarvis said at the time that no good could come of them getting ideas above their station, and his forebodings were soon realized as Accrington marked the new decade by slipping for the first time into Division Four, where they would have to rub shin-pads with the likes of Peterborough and Aldershot. Stanley fans didn't give themselves airs, but they weren't *common*. They might not aspire to the Second Division, but being relegated to the Fourth represented a stigma they feared like poverty. But hardly had the Jarvis household come to terms with this disgrace than worse occurred as the club, plagued by debts and mismanagement, resigned from the Football League in mid-season without even completing its fixtures.

The local fishmonger had once demonstrated for Stan's mum, who was squeamish about such things, the humane method of killing lobsters: you drove a sharp point – he'd used a bradawl – into the creature's nerve centre. The news of Accrington's demise had a similar effect on Stan's dad. 'The Owd Reds' had become a repository for everything he had lost – the mist pouring down off the moors, that girl's thighs going up the top deck of the tram, the blowfly sheen on the bacon in the window of the grocer's – and now this last and seemingly secure refuge had been swept away. Harry Jarvis declined overnight into an alcoholic stupor.

His collapse lasted only a month or so, after which he started an affair with their next-door neighbour and perked up no end, but there was no way of knowing that at the time. Young Stan, who was of course scared stiff, soon discovered that the only way to revive his dad was to recite episodes from the club's glorious past, holding up heroic feats and dastardly deeds from past matches for admiration and contempt. In the course of this therapy Stanley discovered without pride or surprise that he could remember almost every detail of Accrington's record during its last decade in the league, but it was not for another six years – by which time his dad had moved in with the woman next door and Stan out to Hendon Police College – that he attended his first live football match.

He found the experience totally bewildering. Instead of the elegant interaction he'd been led to expect, a meaningful drama with a beginning, middle and an end, proliferating complexities building towards a climax where they were satisfyingly resolved, the game was a depressing, pointless chaos of muddled moves, failed attempts, missed passes and cynical brutality, with no perceptible shape or underlying rhythm, no sense or significance. Stan left at half-time, and didn't even bother to check the final score in the paper next day.

Jarvis got to his feet and tried to concentrate on the matter in hand. It was just a question of going through the motions with this Travis woman and he'd be out of here. Not like Anderson, poor sod. No wonder he was a bit rum, stuck out here in the middle of bloody nowhere with a bunch of oldies well past their sell-by dates, judging by what Tomkins had said. Seriously whiffy. Kids were bad enough, but at least with them it got better. What it must be like having to deal with this lot, knowing that however bad it was today it was going to be worse tomorrow, just plain buggered the imagination.

Still, that was no skin off *his* dick, was it? Reports were what it was all about. Been there, seen this, done that, and here's a file to prove it. Besides, the case was open and shut. There was no question that she'd poisoned herself. The PM had turned up a cocktail comprising the morphine syrup she had been prescribed for pain control, a massive overdose of sleeping tablets she'd nicked from her friend and a few glasses of spirits thrown in for good measure. The why wasn't a problem either. She'd just heard that her cancer was terminal and inoperable, and she had never made any secret of the fact that she did not want to die in hospital. Open and shut, wasn't it?

Even this Rosemary Travis spannering up the works with allegations of murder most foul wouldn't have counted for anything if it hadn't been for the forensic report on the samples taken from the scene. Consistency was the name of the game, as Jarvis liked to tell the new recruits. It didn't matter what story you came up with as long as it all hung together, but if what you said on page 42 clashed with something you'd said on page 24 then you were in dead lumber.

In the present case, fortunately, there was no *substantive discrepancy*. SDs were the bane of every policeman's life. Unless spotted in the early stages, they could turn the most promising case into an embarrassing write-off. This, though, was just a *minor anomaly*. All the ingredients which the pathologist had named as causes of death also figured in the samples of cocoa and medicine which Tomkins had found by the bed. The only problem was that the alcohol – some sort of proprietary liqueur – had been mixed into the morphine syrup, and the sleeping tablets crushed up and dissolved in the cocoa.

There was nothing to say that the deceased hadn't done this herself, of course, but it was unusual. Normally a suicide wouldn't bother mixing the stuff together, they'd just scoff it down and let their stomach do the churning. An MA, then, but no more than that. All Jarvis needed to do was tie up the loose ends, take a statement and then piss off – in time for the other half on the way back with any luck.

'Good afternoon, Inspector.'

The voice was low and pleasant. Jarvis turned round as an elderly woman emerged from the shadows of the hallway. At first he made her about sixty, an estimate which he revised progressively upwards as she moved forward into the light. Well-preserved, though. Good bones, and the worst over for the skin and hair. Look much the same in a thousand years, he thought, like that bloke they dug up from the peat bog.

'Well I never!'

The woman stopped in the centre of the room, staring at Jarvis with an expression of disbelief.

'This is really quite extraordinary! I do hope you won't think I'm being familiar, Inspector, but you bear the most astonishing resemblance to one of my nephews. Rather a feckless lad, young Stuart, although he can charm the birds out of the trees when he wants. He lives in Canada and I haven't seen him for donkey's years. Well, now! I don't know, I really don't!'

Anderson came in, accompanied by a burly woman in her thirties wearing a pair of shapeless blue overalls. He gave Jarvis an ingratiating smile.

'May I introduce my sister Letitia, Inspector?'

The woman in overalls nodded at Jarvis, who raised his eyebrows and inclined his head politely. Anderson took the elderly woman by the arm and led her to the chair.

'And this,' he said, 'is Miss Rosemary Travis.'

CHAPTER 8

'Miss Travis, the officers who responded to the 999 call last week reported that you made a number of allegations concerning Mrs Davenport's tragic death. Now under the circumstances it would be perfectly natural if you had said things which you perhaps didn't really mean. If that's the case, just say so and this need go no further.'

They stood in a ring, Jarvis, Anderson and his sister, looking down at the elderly lady sitting bolt upright on the edge of the armchair. To mitigate the effect of an interrogation, Jarvis seated himself on the wooden stool which stood in front of the writing-desk.

'It must have been a terrible shock for you,' he suggested in a kindly tone.

Rosemary Travis looked him in the eye.

'Murder is always unpleasant, Inspector. So much the more so when the victim was one's best friend.'

'Chuck it, Travis!' growled the woman in overalls.

She grinned coquettishly at Jarvis.

'Brains in their bums,' she said.

Anderson put his arm around his sister's shoulders.

'I think perhaps you should go and see how lunch is coming along, Letty,' he muttered.

The woman flinched.

'There's no need for that, William.'

The arm encircling her tightened a fraction.

'I believe there is.'

'It's spam sandwiches with cold baked beans. What can go wrong?'

Anderson smiled thinly.

'Nevertheless, I feel quite strongly that you should go.'

'But I don't want to.'

They stared at each other. After some time the woman's breathing became loud and laboured, and her left cheek began to twitch uncontrollably. Anderson smiled and withdrew his restraining arm. His sister turned and ran out of the room, slamming the door loudly behind her.

Anderson sighed and shook his head.

'Poor Letitia!'

He looked at Jarvis.

'Our father was exceptionally intelligent, our mother strikingly beautiful. In an ideal world, each child would have received a portion of these gifts. As it was, I inherited Papa's brains *and* Mamma's looks, while Letitia got the latter's muddle-through-somehow mind installed in a superficially feminized version of Pater's burly bod. It is an unenviable not to say frankly repellent combination, and one which perhaps goes some way towards explaining her often startlingly abrupt manners. My apologies for the interruption, Inspector.'

He drifted over to the writing-desk and refilled his tumbler. Jarvis turned to the elderly lady perched on the edge of the armchair. Her expression was full of mild determination, but held no clue as to her feelings about the scene which they had just witnessed.

Jarvis got out his notebook, turned to a blank page and licked the lead of his pencil.

'Right, let's have it.'

Rosemary Travis frowned politely.

'I beg your pardon, Inspector?'

'What makes you think Mrs Davenport was murdered?' Jarvis demanded.

'I don't think so,' Rosemary replied.

Jarvis narrowed his eyes.

'You don't?'

'Certainly not. I *know* she was murdered. And so you jolly well should too. The evidence is clear enough, for heaven's sake.'

Anderson gave Jarvis a look which said 'Now do you see what I mean?' Perhaps he has a point at that, thought Jarvis with a sudden flash of irritation. He'd been willing to give the old biddy the benefit of the doubt, but enough was enough.

'What evidence?' he snapped.

'Why, the morphine syrup and the cocoa, of course! I managed – with some difficulty, I might say – to per-suade one of your officers to take them away with him. Frank, I believe his name was. The near-sighted one from the Isle of Wight. I assumed they would have been analysed by now, and the results communicated to whoever's in charge.'

She peered at Jarvis as though struck by a sudden doubt.

'You *are* in charge, aren't you?'

Jarvis knew that the way he was gaping suggested he wasn't in charge of his wits, never mind the investigation. Although Frank – 'call me Franklin' – Tomkins had indeed been born and raised in Newport, he wouldn't have admitted under torture that it was the one on the Isle of Wight rather than the Kentucky bank of the Ohio River, still less that the 'shades' he affected were in fact prescription sunglasses.

'The items in question mentioned were duly passed to our forensic department for routine examination,' said Jarvis, pulling himself together with an effort.

'With what result?'

Jarvis took refuge in his notebook for a moment.

'The cocoa in the mug contained nitrazepam, commonly known by the trade name Mogadon. The medicine bottle contained a mixture of morphine syrup, as specified on the label, and a proprietary liqueur known as Bols Blue Curaçao.'

Anderson grunted.

'Personally I prefer this cask-strength Ardbeg '73. The distillery may have closed, but its spirit lives on. Sure you won't indulge, Inspector?'

Rosemary smoothed the skirt over her lower limbs.

'Well, there's your evidence,' she remarked tartly. 'The question now is who did it, and I warn you that the solution will be a supreme test of your detective abilities. All the residents visited Dorothy's room that evening to wish her farewell, and in the mêlée which followed Miss Davis's appearance it would have been a simple matter for any of them to have added the lethal combination of sleeping tablets to the cocoa and alcohol to the morphine syrup.'

Jarvis clacked his teeth together a few times. Preston North End 1, Accrington Stanley 1. Billy Duff's goal saved the day for the Reds, but Preston went on to win the replay. They'd *wept*, him and his dad.

'Who's Miss Davis?' he murmured.

'My sister,' replied Anderson. 'Letty affects our mother's maiden name in order, and I quote, to "make a statement".'

Rosemary gave a discreet cough, as though to call the proceedings to order.

'George Channing is the only suspect who can be excluded at this stage,' she continued, 'having been confined to his bed following the unfortunate incident involving Mr Anderson's dog. We are thus left with a total of seven suspects. A very satisfactory number, don't you agree, Inspector? Large enough to allow a sufficient variety of possibilities without being, as dear Dorothy once put it, *unnecessarily* vast.'

Jarvis squirmed about on his stool, which seemed to be growing harder by the moment.

'Look, Miss Travis, there's nothing to suggest that those pills were taken from your room by anyone other than . . . '

'Oh, I shouldn't pursue that avenue of inquiry, if I were you,' Rosemary interrupted. 'None of our rooms can be locked, and I only use the sleeping tablets very infrequently. Any of the suspects could therefore have taken them, possibly some time ago, without my being aware of the fact. Bearing that in mind, I suggest we concentrate our attention on the question of the blue curaçao.'

'My dear Miss Travis . . . ' boomed Jarvis.

'Now at one time, it is true, we used to be offered a glass of sherry at Christmas and suchlike festivities, but that custom has long since lapsed. Mr Anderson will bear me out when I say that at present the residents have no access to alcoholic beverages at all. That being so, the first problem we must resolve is how the murderer obtained a supply of the exotic liqueur which he – or she – used to intensify the narcotic action of the morphine syrup to a fatal degree.'

Feeling an urgent need to assert his authority, to say nothing of giving his backside a rest, Jarvis rose to his feet. He towered over the elderly woman, swaying back and forth in the manner cultivated by the constabulary for the purposes of impressing the populace.

'I fully recognize how painful it must be for you to accept that Mrs Davenport took her own life,' he stated. 'Nevertheless, the fact remains that there is not a single shred of evidence to suggest otherwise. As far as the curaçao is concerned, we naturally made inquiries as soon as the forensic report revealed its presence in the sample of morphine syrup. It transpired that this liqueur is among those kept on the premises for the use of the owners.'

Anderson walked over to the escritoire. He lifted a wide-bottomed bottle and swirled the viscid blue contents around.

'My sister's poison,' he said. 'I'd as soon drink meths myself.'

'I believe this room isn't locked?' Jarvis prompted.

Rosemary held up her hand like a pupil in class.

'Surely the important point, Inspector . . .'

'No, no,' Anderson replied. 'Although my little sanctum is theoretically off-bounds to residents, it would have been quite simple for Mrs Davenport to sneak in here and filch some booze with a view to ceasing upon the midnight with no pain. The only mystery is why, with such an array of rare – and in some cases unobtainable – malts at her disposal, she should have chosen this appalling blue muck.'

'Precisely!' cried Rosemary.

Struggling to her feet, she grasped Jarvis's arm.

'That is the key to the whole mystery! Don't you see, Inspector? Even supposing that Dorothy had been capable of breaking in here and stealing spirits – and anyone who knew her will tell you how absurd that hypothesis is – we have to explain the remarkable coincidence that of all the drinks available she happened to select the only one which will not reveal its presence when added to morphine syrup *because they are the same colour*.'

She stared intensely at Jarvis.

'If Dorothy had deliberately chosen to put an end to her life, she would have had no need to dissolve the sleeping pills in her cocoa or carefully disguise the fact that her medicine had been adulterated with alcohol. There is only one possible reason why anyone should go to such extraordinary lengths, and that is to conceal the fact that Dorothy's death was not suicide but cold-blooded premeditated murder!'

'Or to draw attention to it,' said Jarvis.

They stared at each other.

'I'm afraid I don't understand,' Rosemary replied in a haughty tone.

Jarvis turned to Anderson.

'If you don't mind, sir, I'd like a word with Miss Travis in private.'

Anderson drew Jarvis to one side.

'You're not starting to take her seriously, I hope?' he murmured. 'If so, let me slip you a quick *verb. sap*. Letty may be a foul-mouthed slag who might be compared to a brick outhouse to that edifice's advantage, but believe me, she has this lady's number. Like all those who deceive themselves before practising on others, it's a tangled web Miss Travis weaves. Should you become ensnared in it, Inspector, you would become the laughing-stock of your colleagues and superiors.'

'I'll thank you to allow me to carry out my duties as I see fit, sir,' Jarvis replied stiffly.

Anderson shrugged.

'Very well!' he sighed.

He refilled his glass and slouched out, closing the door with an exaggerated care in pointed contrast to his sister's abrupt exit.

'Now I *do* hope you're not going to allow yourself to be deceived into suspecting the staff,' Rosemary told Jarvis. 'Even discounting those purists who would exclude such a solution on principle, it seems safe to assume that any suspect whose guilt seems as blatant as the Andersons in the present case is bound to be a red herring.'

Jarvis grasped the bridge of his nose between finger and thumb. Give me strength, he thought. Don't let me hit an old lady.

'May I remind you, Miss Travis,' he said, 'that this is real life, not some thriller?'

'Thriller?' Rosemary queried acidly. 'My dear Inspector, I hope you don't think for a moment that I would concern myself with any such rubbish. My only interest is in the classic English detective story, with its unique blend of logic and fair play. There is no room for sloppy guesswork or vulgar sensationalism. If you observe the rules, spot the clues and make the appropriate deductions, you should be able to arrive at the correct solution.'

'In real life,' Jarvis continued implacably, 'poison is the least common method of murder, accounting for less than six per cent of all cases.'

'Of the cases that come to light, perhaps. But who is to say how many homicidal poisonings are successfully passed off as illness, accidents or – as in the present instance – suicide?'

Jarvis struck his forehead with the heel of his hand.

'For the love of . . . !'

He stared into space for some time, running over the results and league positions for January 1958. Eighteen thousand turned out to watch them draw one all at Bury. Happy days!

'I am a police officer, Miss Travis,' he declared at last.

'I know that,' Rosemary replied brightly.

'As such, I cannot conduct an investigation on the basis of hearsay, innuendo, rumour or fantasy. I require evidence. And as I have already said, there is no evidence whatsoever to suggest that Mrs Dorothy Davenport did not take her own life.'

'But why should Dorothy go to such pains to disguise the lethal combination of drugs mixed into her cocoa and medicine?'

'I don't believe she did.'

'Exactly!' Rosemary exclaimed triumphantly. 'Then who did?'

'You.'

They confronted each other for a long moment. Then a smile of pure pleasure lit up the woman's frail, wrinkled features.

'Do you know, Inspector, you're not such a fool as

you look! How clever of you to notice that I had deliberately excluded myself from the list of suspects.'

Jarvis hid his face in his hands. I don't believe this, he thought.

'I don't believe this,' he said.

Rosemary frowned.

'We can't afford to exclude any possibilities at this stage, however unlikely they may appear. Even George Channing's innocence should perhaps not be taken for granted. One might argue that the very fact that his alibi seems unbreakable in itself constitutes grounds for suspicion, and his room is of course next door to the victim's. Secret passages are always a tendentious topic, but I think one might be regarded as permissible in a house such as this. On the other hand, the hideous injuries which Channing sustained might seem to preclude . . . '

'What injuries?'

' . . . and of course his motive is a good deal less obvious than, say, the Andersons'.'

Jarvis felt the way he had on the never-to-be-forgotten day when Accrington creamed Stockport 4 nil to stay in the promotion race, and his dad let him drink the sediment out of his bottles of White Label. The pitch was tilting, the goalposts moving, the ref nowhere to be seen.

'Who is this Channing?' he demanded truculently. 'What happened to him?'

Rosemary waved vaguely.

'Don't let's get off the point, Inspector. The only aspect of poor Channing's ordeal which need concern us is that it might appear to give him a perfect alibi . . . '

'*What happened to him?*'

' . . . intended to divert suspicion from the real cul-
prit, who has cleverly covered his – or her – tracks
by . . . '

'FOR THE LOVE OF GOD, WOMAN, WHAT HAPPENED?'

Rosemary Travis threw up her hands in exasperation.

'Oh really, Inspector! Since you persistently refuse to
listen to my advice, you can jolly well go and find out
for yourself.'

CHAPTER 9

'Tell you the truth, I rather fancied a career in the police myself at one time,' said Miss Davis, leading the way upstairs.

'And I'm sure you would have been a great credit to the force,' Jarvis replied gallantly.

Miss Davis tittered.

'Either that or the Army,' she went on as they reached the landing. 'It was not to be, however. As the runt female of the litter, I let myself be talked into taking up the teaching game instead.'

She barked a laugh.

'Not that it made much difference in the end. The parents apparently thought of education as a suitably ladylike activity, like being a nurse, only more genteel. Maybe it used to be, too, when there was proper discipline at home and the kids came to you already broken in. These days the only thing you have a hope of teaching most of them is that you *don't fuck with the system*.'

'Well this is it,' murmured Jarvis.

'And though I have no wish to brag,' Miss Davis went on, 'I turned out to be a natural.'

They came to a doorway opening into what looked like a walk-in cupboard.

'The only thing I really missed was the uniform,' she

concluded reminiscently. 'That and being able to go all the way. Know what I mean?'

Inside the narrow cubicle were two plywood doors with cheap gilt handles. Miss Davis opened the one to the left and ushered Jarvis inside. An expanse of flowery-patterned wallpaper rose to an inordinately high ceiling. A grimy sash-window overlooked an over-grown walled garden where a large dog was secured by a length of orange rope. The air was as cold and still as marble.

'That's where she breathed her last,' Miss Davis remarked, pointing to a metal bed-frame in the opposite corner. 'Choked, rather. Messy business, but all part of a day's work round here. And guess who has to get down on her bended knees and do the necessary? God forbid my precious brother should sully his fingers. I mean pul*eeease*!'

Jarvis surveyed the personal effects gathering dust on top of the chest of drawers. He picked up a small bevelled cone of polished stone, which proved on closer inspection to be a souvenir of Land's End. Rosemary Travis had warned him that if he asked to speak to George Channing directly the Andersons would claim that he wasn't well enough to receive visitors. She had therefore suggested that he tell them he wished to search Mrs Davenport's room, as was only natural in the circumstances, and then find some pretext for going next door.

Despite his reluctance to take advice from outsiders on professional matters, Jarvis had been forced to con-cede the wisdom of this. The last thing he wanted to do was to get on the wrong side of someone like this Anderson, who was related to the local MP and reportedly had the ear of various big noises on the council. He put the statuette down beside a set of miniature bottles in a wooden case and ran one finger along the top of the chest of drawers, tracing a straight line in the gathering dust. A long hair looped up and curled itself about his finger, glinting in the dull light. He brushed it away with a shudder. He'd seen the police photos and even attended the PM, yet it was only now that the fact of Dorothy Davenport's death came home to him.

In the centre of the room, Miss Davis was going through a brief but energetic workout, stretching and bending alternately to either side. Jarvis pointed to the dead woman's possessions.

'Aren't you going to clear this stuff out?' he demanded brusquely. 'Move in another paying customer?'

'Only wish we could,' Miss Davis puffed.

Jarvis opened the wooden case and took out a tiny replica of a green gin bottle. He unscrewed the top and turned it up. A drop of brackish water fell to the back of his hand.

'Recession biting?' he suggested sarcastically. 'Bottom fallen out of the caring market, has it?'

Miss Davis laughed.

'You must be joking! We've got people practically beating the door down, they're that desperate to get rid.'

Jarvis replaced the miniature in its case and picked up a dusty bouquet of dried poppies.

'The problem is William,' Miss Davis panted, scissoring her arms from side to side. 'He was spoilt rotten as a child, needless to say. No spunk, no gumption.'

One of the dead flowers, disturbed by Jarvis's

probing finger, broke free of the bouquet and fell. Borne on currents of air created by the flurry of activity at the centre of the room, it drifted laterally in a series of twirling spirals before coming to rest near the head of the bed.

'Only a psycho could actually *enjoy* this work,' Miss Davis grunted, 'but what the hell, it's a living. Don't kill the golden goose is the way I look at it. But William can hardly wait.'

As Jarvis bent to pick up the poppy, a gleam caught his eye. He extended two fingers and grasped the slithery scrap of torn plastic.

'And what will become of you?' he murmured. 'Back to teaching, is it?'

There was some black lettering on the plastic. Holding it up to the window, Jarvis read '50 ml disposable syr . . .'.

'Over my dead body!' snorted Miss Davis.

Jarvis put the scrap of plastic into his wallet.

'If you still fancied a job with the police,' he said, 'something might be arranged.'

Miss Davis ceased her exertions.

'Really?' she breathed.

'We're always on the lookout for people with the right mentality,' Jarvis told her. 'You can teach everything else, but you can't teach that. You've either got it or you haven't.'

Miss Davis's eyes grew wider.

'And you think I have?'

Jarvis winked.

'I feel it. In my bones.'

Miss Davis blushed.

'Cor,' she said.

'Now let's just have a quick look next door,' Jarvis went on briskly. 'In case there's a secret passage.'

Miss Davis looked flustered.

'Secret passage?'

'I think one might be regarded as permissible in a house such as this,' he announced airily, heading for the door.

Miss Davis caught him up.

'You can't!'

'Whyever not? You haven't got anything to hide, have you?'

She stared at him in silence for some time, then shrugged.

'I'd better ask William.'

Jarvis tapped the side of his nose with his forefinger.

'Rule Number One,' he said. 'What your superior officer doesn't find out didn't happen. Right?'

'Yes, but . . .'

'*Right?*'

Miss Davis nodded.

'Right,' she said.

Jarvis opened the door and stepped inside. At first sight, the room seemed a mirror image of the one next door: the same miscellaneous assortment of third-hand furniture, the same oppressive volume of chilly grey light, the same sense of desolation and decay. The only difference Jarvis noticed at first was that the lower pane of the window had been replaced by a rectangle of plywood. Then he heard a low moan, and realized with a shock that what lay on the bed was not just a mattress but a man, bound to the frame at the wrists and ankles.

'Doctor's orders,' Miss Davis explained, hurriedly undoing the webbing which bound the man to the bed-frame. 'Wouldn't lie still, would you, George? Kept reopening his wounds, so we had to restrain him.'

The elderly man moved his arms and legs feebly, groaning through his clenched, toothless gums. A series of long shallow cuts extended from the temple to the chin on one side of his face, while on the other there were two deep gashes which had been stitched. His hands and arms were heavily bandaged. The rest of his body was concealed by the covers.

'What happened?' Jarvis asked.

Miss Davis took up a position at the head of the bed.

'Had an accident, didn't you, George? Tripped and fell out of the window.'

Ignoring her, Channing turned his head to look at Jarvis.

'They set the dog on me,' he said.

'We never!' shouted Miss Davis.

She bent over the bed, fist raised. Jarvis grasped her arm and led her away.

'If you're to be any use to us in the police,' he hissed, 'you must learn never to interrupt an officer when he's interviewing a witness!'

'But the old bastard just fibbed himself!'

Jarvis nodded earnestly.

'You don't think I *believe* him, do you?' he whispered.

Miss Davis gawked. Jarvis gave her a playful nudge.

'Rule Number Two is let 'em talk. The more he says, the easier it is to spot the inconsistencies and trap him in his own contradictions.'

A smile spread slowly across Miss Davis's face. Leaning back slightly, she punched Jarvis on the shoulder.

'Oooooh, you are a one!' she said.

Surreptitiously rubbing his aching shoulder, Jarvis sat down on the edge of the bed.

'Now then,' he said, 'what was that about a dog?'

A scornful smile appeared on the man's ravaged face.

'Jerry couldn't hold me in '44. Got as far as Ostend that time, and would have made it back to Blighty if I hadn't been turned in by some bloody Belgian. Whistling in the street, you see, hands in pockets. Not done *sur le continong*, it seems.'

He pointed one bandaged hand at the broken window.

'Worked the pane loose and climbed out. Managed to get down from the ledge in one piece, then the hound got me.'

'And you've been kept tied up here ever since?' Jarvis murmured.

The man nodded.

'Medic came that afternoon, patched me up.'

He laughed soundlessly.

'Worried I might die on them. Wouldn't look good, he said. Got the wind up about old Davvers, too.'

'Mrs Davenport?'

The bandaged hand beckoned. Jarvis bent down over the pillow and the man's humid breath billowed in his ear.

'Wall's like paper. Hear every word.'

Jarvis nodded.

'The morning they found the body, before the police got here, I heard Anderson talking to someone in there,' Channing went on in a sibilant whisper. 'Couldn't make out the other voice, but it must have been . . .'

His eyes swivelled towards the figure in blue overalls standing by the window, ostentatiously not listening.

'Anderson was in a bit of a panic. Man's a dipso, of course. Always go to pieces at the first sign of trouble. Kept wittering away about how the police would be there any minute. Then something about getting rid of something at all costs. Miss Davis must have asked him where, and Anderson says, "In a bloody haystack." '

'A haystack?' repeated Jarvis.

'Then she said something else, and he said, "Well, we'll just have to make sure they don't get a chance to speak to her." Then he laughed and said, "Don't worry, I'll handle them. The police are such clods." '

The man lay back on the pillow, exhausted. Jarvis stood up.

'Thank you,' he said.

He pointed to the wrist and ankle restraints.

'I don't really think those are necessary any more,' he told Miss Davis.

'Not if he'll be good,' she shrugged. 'Will you be good, George?'

Jarvis took her arm.

'I'm sure he will,' he said, guiding her to the door.

'What did he say?' Miss Davis demanded as soon as they were outside.

Jarvis shrugged negligently.

'Oh, nothing much. This and that. You know.'

This could be it, he thought as they started along the corridor. The one he'd always dreamed about, the one that got you on TV telling some prat in a mac how it felt. He imagined opening his morning paper to find a headline reading 'HELL HOME HORROR – Exclusive Pictures and Interview with Detective Chief Superintendent "Accrington" Stanley Jarvis'. Then he blinked, and the next moment the whole thing looked as insubstantial as the world-shattering insights Tomkins tended to come out with after the fifth bottle of Bud or Schlitz or whatever it was that week.

No way, Stan, he told himself. The last thing he could afford to do was chance his arm on something that could blow up in his face and leave him without a leg to stand on if it subsequently turned out that he'd put his foot in it. This Miss Davis might come across with a bit of flattery, but her brother was considerably less of a soft touch, and well-connected with it. You couldn't risk going up against people like that on the basis of a few ambiguous overheard phrases and the melodramatic fantasies of the dead woman's best friend.

Jarvis was no longer totally convinced that Rosemary Travis had adulterated the cocoa and morphine syrup herself, but that didn't mean she was someone you could put in the witness-box if you wanted to reach retirement age with your reputation intact. Reluctantly he let the dreams of fame and fortune fade. In his heart he had always known that he was not destined for such things any more than the football club after which he had been named. Accrington fans regarded titles and cups as slightly swanky, suitable for folk in Blackburn or Burnley, but not their style. Like them, Jarvis knew his place.

They had almost reached the landing when they heard Anderson yelling 'Letty! Letty!'

Miss Davis broke into a run, with Jarvis close behind. As they reached the bottom of the stairs, Anderson appeared from his office. He pointed to the front door, which was wide open.

'Hargreaves is loose!'

Miss Davis's eyes narrowed.

'The bitch. I'll fucking spay her.'

Anderson smiled urbanely at Jarvis.

'Sorry about this, Inspector! A minor domestic crisis, such as will happen from time to time in even the best-regulated households.'

The smile vanished as he turned to his sister.

'You take the north side, I'll check the paddock. She can't have gone far.'

The front door clacked shut and footsteps scurried away over the gravel. Jarvis paused to check his appearance in the mirror at the foot of the stairs. He'd have been perfect on TV, too, he thought with a twinge of regret. He looked the part: solid, sound, dogged but fundamentally uninspired. People would have trusted him. That Jarvis, they'd have said, he's all right. Shame there aren't more like him in the force.

'We're ready for you, Inspector.'

He spun around to find Rosemary Travis looking at him from a doorway near by.

'This way!' she said.

Jarvis walked past her into the lounge. The other residents were all in their places: Weatherby sitting by the fireplace reading *The Times*, Charles Symes and Grace Lebon bent over a jigsaw puzzle, Samuel Rossiter muttering into the telephone, Belinda Scott lightly touching the keys of the piano, Purvey nodding over his book.

'So, here we are,' Rosemary remarked brightly, 'gathered together in the lounge of this isolated country house to face the detective's probing questions. One of us is guilty, but which? Can the sleuth succeed in unmasking the murderer before he – or she – strikes again?'

The seven faces gazed expectantly at Jarvis.

'Yes, well . . . ' he said.

He licked his lips.

'The thing is . . . ' he said.

He consulted the marble clock on the mantelpiece, which read ten past four.

'I'd like to ask you each a few questions,' he said.

He pointed at the skinny woman bent over the keyboard of the piano, her shrivelled body hinting at vanished beauty like the chrysalis of a butterfly condemned to live its brief life backwards.

'I'll start with you,' said Stanley Jarvis masterfully.

CHAPTER 10

By the time Anderson reappeared in the lounge some twenty minutes later, Jarvis had spoken to all the residents except the errant Mrs Hargreaves. With the exception of Alfred Purvey, who was definitely a few stamps short of the first-class rate, they proved to be considerably less gaga than Jarvis had feared. Unfortunately it was Purvey who had come up with the only substantive piece of new information, which virtually destroyed its value as evidence.

Surrounded as he was by formless, menacing uncertainties, Purvey left nothing to chance in those aspects of his life which he could control. His 'jabs' were the most significant of these. The regular regime of insulin injections had come to provide a certainty on which not only his life but also his sanity to some extent depended, and he was fanatically precise about everything relating to it. On the other hand, he was convinced that his tenure at Eventide Lodge was entirely dependent on the goodwill of his 'hosts', and he was therefore very reluctant to make any fuss about what was in any case a very minor matter: the disappearance of his syringes at some point in the course of the previous week.

If true, this removed the basic stumbling block to

Rosemary Travis's theory of murder, which she herself, for all her much-vaunted prowess in the matter of detective stories, had completely overlooked. If Dorothy Davenport had not intended to kill herself, she would have taken no more than the prescribed dose of her medicine, and even in combination with alcohol and sleeping tablets this was not sufficient to cause death. What it *would* do was ensure that the victim fell into a deep sleep, thus enabling a potential murderer to inject a quantity of morphine consistent with that revealed by the post-mortem. And if some eagle-eyed pathologist happened to notice the puncture mark, Mrs Davenport's medical record would reveal that she had received a number of injections over the past few weeks in the course of the tests she had undergone.

In theory then, Purvey's testimony, together with the fragment from the plastic wrapping of the syringe which Jarvis had discovered under the victim's bed, cleared the way for him to open a full-scale murder investigation. But in theory only. The simple fact was that no evidence Alfred Purvey might give was likely to carry any weight with Jarvis's superiors, still less a jury. Jarvis shuddered to think what a sarcastic QC would do to Purvey if he got a chance to cross-examine him. Clearly the testimony of a mind so pathetically at variance with reality could not be credited for a single instant. On the contrary, the implication had to be that the surer Alfred Purvey was about anything, the less likely it was to be true.

This was particularly galling in view of the fact that Purvey had not only noticed the loss of the syringe, but had seen the person who had taken it from his room.

'I thought at first that I was dreaming,' he said with

an apologetic smile. 'The door was wide open – not that I ever shut it completely. One doesn't want to appear discourteous . . . '

'Go on,' said Jarvis, cutting quickly through what he had by now identified as a recurrent closed loop.

'The curtains were still drawn, and as the room in which I am staying is on the western side of the house, it is rather dark in the mornings – not that I wish to complain, of course! Heaven knows, it's only too good of them to put me up at all . . . '

'Go on.'

'I noticed a woman moving about. What with the poor light and my own drowsiness I was unable to identify the intruder – although that is of course a wholly inappropriate word in the circumstances, implying as it does . . . '

'*Go on!*'

'Then I must have dosed off again. When I woke, the room was empty and the door ajar. I got out of bed and found that one of the syringes which I keep on top of the chest of drawers was missing.'

To cap the unfavourable impression which would be made by Purvey's repeated references to falling asleep and dreaming, it transpired that he had no idea which day these events had occurred. It was thus without any great hopes that Jarvis had asked his next question.

'So you have no idea who took your syringe?'

'Oh yes,' Purvey replied simply. 'It was Miss Davis.'

It took Jarvis a moment to master his emotion.

'How do you know?' he asked casually.

'Well, by . . . by the smell.'

'Smell?' echoed Jarvis.

'Of drink,' Purvey explained.

Jarvis stared at him. Purvey blinked mildly.

'Spirituous liquor,' he said. 'If one has been strictly TT all one's life, as I have, there's no mistaking the nauseous odour. As I say, the intruder was a woman, and of course none of my fellow guests have any access to alcoholic beverages. Not of course that I wish to give the impression of making judgements on those who have been so good as to take me in . . . '

'Ah, here you are, Inspector!' cried Anderson, appearing in the doorway. 'I hope my little flock haven't been trying your patience too much.'

He fixed Rosemary with a keen gaze.

'I take it this was your idea, Miss Travis?'

Jarvis got to his feet.

'It was mine,' he snapped. 'Even we *clods* in the police get ideas of our own from time to time.'

He had expected Anderson to react to hearing his sneering words quoted back at him, but he merely shrugged.

'I'm sure you do, Inspector, but I was in fact referring to the episode involving Mrs Hargreaves.'

'Where is she?' Rosemary asked.

'I'm so sorry you've been subjected to this unnecessary delay,' Anderson murmured to Jarvis. 'Please don't let us detain you any longer. You must be anxious to go.'

Rosemary pushed her way between the two men.

'Where's Mavis?' she demanded. 'Is she all right?'

Anderson regarded her coldly.

'Mrs Hargreaves is in the capable hands of my sister, Miss Travis. She is as well as can be expected.'

Turning his back on her, he led Jarvis to the door.

'The whole thing was my fault for neglecting to lock

up properly after letting you in,' he explained in an undertone. 'Normally we keep all the hatches firmly battened down lest the fauna get loose and do themselves an injury. Old Weatherby fell down the ha-ha last year and was in plaster for six weeks. You wouldn't believe the pain and inconvenience we were put to. Time was you could get some great gormless strapping country lass in to do for them, but these days they all want minimum wages and National Insurance stamps and a week's paid holiday in Tenerife.'

'Where did you find her?'

'Hargreaves?' Anderson replied breezily. 'Letitia treed her in the copper beech on the east lawn.'

'You didn't have to use the dog this time, then?'

Anderson gave him a sharp look.

'Have they been telling you about Channing?'

He sighed and shook his head.

'A typical example of the way they personalize everything. The results can be quite alarming until you learn to decode them. Symes, for instance, suffers from incontinence caused by an anal tumour which causes him a certain amount of discomfort. Since there is a long waiting-list for the operation, we have to put up with the mess and stench as best we can. Mr Symes's response has been to accuse my sister of cauterizing his rectum with a red-hot poker. Like Miss Travis, he prefers to ascribe his suffering to individual villainy rather than to the shortcomings of the health service and the workings of a fate which is simply indifferent to human misery.'

He led Jarvis into the hallway.

'As for Channing, he has no one but himself to blame for what happened. The man's an obsessive escapologist. He managed to get away from some POW camp during the war and has been bragging about it ever since. Last week he decided to show us all that he'd lost none of the old skills. Unfortunately he happened to choose a moment when my pet was stretching his legs in the grounds. The worst of it is that his adventure seems to have started a trend. Now they all want to have a go.'

He unlocked the front door and held it open.

'I would ask you to stay for lunch, Inspector, but Letitia's catering, although perfectly nourishing, is not the sort of thing you'd invite someone to. Give my respects to the Chief Constable, should you happen to bump into him. We met at a charity dinner it must be, let's see, three years ago now?'

'You haven't spoken to Mrs Hargreaves yet,' said a voice behind them.

'Go back to the lounge, Miss Travis,' Anderson called sternly without glancing round.

Rosemary grasped the sleeve of Jarvis's overcoat.

'You must speak to Mavis Hargreaves!'

'She won't be able to tell him anything he hasn't already heard fifty times from the others,' Anderson retorted dismissively.

Rosemary looked straight into Jarvis's eyes.

'If you leave now, I will be the next to die,' she told him. 'I hope you will at least investigate *that* properly.'

Jarvis stared back, shaken by the utter conviction of her tone. He had enough experience of people lying to him to know that Rosemary Travis was speaking the truth – or what she believed to be the truth.

'Mrs Hargreaves is in no condition to speak to anyone,' Anderson remarked.

'What have you done to her?' Rosemary cried. 'Let me see her! Let me see her!'

'It's all right,' Jarvis told her. 'I'll make sure she's all right, and I'll listen to anything she has to tell me.'

He turned to Anderson.

'Where is she?'

Anderson shook his head.

'Letty is just applying some soothing embrocation to the contusions which Mrs Hargreaves sustained in the course of her escapade,' he said. 'If you care to wait in my office, I'll bring her to you.'

Deliberately avoiding Rosemary Travis's eye, Jarvis crossed the hall to the book-lined room he had entered what seemed like an age ago. He was prepared to back her up to the extent of defying Anderson over this particular issue, but that was as far as he could go on the basis of the information he had. Voices heard through a partition wall, a scrap of plastic, a figure half-glimpsed by someone who might have been dreaming – these were all nice bits of circumstantial decoration, but they were no use to him without some crucial piece of evidence to tie the whole thing together. He couldn't even imagine what that might be, still less believe that this Mrs Hargreaves was magically going to come up with it. That was as soft as his adolescent fantasies about Accrington winning the FA Cup.

The furthest they'd ever got was the third round, but each year young Stanley told himself that this time it might be a different story. The fascination of the Cup was that past reputations and current form counted for nothing. It was all down to what happened on the day. In practice, of course, that was largely determined by the skill and experience of the players, which in turn reflected the financial standing of the clubs concerned, which was dependent on their ability to attract the rewards that success brings with it. The competition was thus a faithful model of British society: supposedly accessible to all comers of talent and ability, in fact dominated by a few established clans who could now unashamedly flaunt a natural superiority which had been demonstrated in fair and open competition.

This had given Stan's daydreams an extra edge. When he visualized the Accrington team striding out into the terrifying expanses of Wembley, the odds they faced were comparable to those which had governed his father's life, and that of everyone they knew. Their opponents, as befitted their symbolic status, wore varying strips and assumed a variety of aliases, until the day Stan heard his dad sounding off about someone – it turned out to be the woman he later took up with – acting 'like a bloody Chelsea débutante'. From that moment on the names of Manchester United and Liverpool were heard no more. It was always the snooty Blues with whom the Owd Reds marched out to do battle in Stanley's imagination. Mighty Chelsea, flying high in Division One versus lowly Accrington, struggling to survive in the lower reaches of the Third. All in all, the lads might have been forgiven for conceding defeat in advance and putting the train fare towards a decent striker for the next season.

Nor did anything in the first half suggest that the result would be anything but wholly predictable. By the time the whistle blew Accrington were trailing by two goals to nil, and it could easily have been twice that if Chelsea had taken a few of the chances which had been handed them on a plate. But in the second half the whole tenor of the game abruptly changed.

It all began when Chelsea's central defender scored an own goal with an ill-judged back pass. The London side recovered quickly, coming back with another goal which was disallowed on a blatantly incorrect off-side decision which so upset the Chelsea players that two of them were booked. When one subsequently expressed his frustration by bringing down his opposite number, he was promptly sent off, and Stanley's centre-forward scored from the spot to level the scores. But although the Blues were down to ten men, this seemed to concentrate their formidable abilities, and by the end of the first period of extra time Accrington had not only failed to score the winning goal but had themselves been saved by the woodwork on no less than three occasions. There were now only five minutes left before the final whistle blew, five minutes for Accrington to achieve the glory which had always eluded them and write their name in the history books for ever . . .

'Right, Inspector!'

For a moment Jarvis thought that Rosemary Travis had come to hound him with some new and ingenious theory, but when he looked around he found that the speaker had been Mr Anderson. Beside him stood a plump woman in a loud print dress who wound a strand of pale blonde hair around her finger as she gazed distractedly at Jarvis.

'There's lots of rape about,' she said dreamily, waddling towards him.

Jarvis gaped at her. This was one complaint he hadn't heard from the other residents. As the woman approached, Jarvis noticed that her right cheek was puffy and discoloured.

'Fields of it, everywhere,' she went on. 'And such beautiful tits, too.'

'Too?' Jarvis echoed feebly.

Mavis Hargreaves nodded.

'A pair, yes. *Mating*, I shouldn't wonder.'

She touched Jarvis's arm.

'It was worth it just to be outside again.'

Another loony, thought Jarvis, the last embers of hope dying in his heart. They were into injury time now, the referee consulting his watch, only seconds left for Accrington to produce the impossible winner from nowhere.

'I've been asking everyone here about the evening Mrs Davenport died,' he recited dully. 'I don't suppose you recall anything unusual happening?'

Mavis Hargreaves gawked at him with a witless grin.

'Anything at all,' Jarvis stressed, trying to let her off easily, 'however insignificant it may seem.'

'Only the cocoa.'

Jarvis jerked his head up.

'Cocoa?'

The woman tittered.

'I was going to take the wrong mug,' she said. 'Would you credit it? I always use the pink one, but that night I went to take the dark blue, which was Dorothy's, of course. It was thinking about her going, I suppose, that got me muddled. Luckily Miss Davis put me right. "Not that one," she says, "that's a special treat for our Dorothy. We've put in an extra dose of sugar to speed the parting guest." '

'She must be concussed,' Anderson whispered

124

urgently to Jarvis. 'Even by her standards, this is complete idiocy. I'd better call the doctor.'

Mavis Hargreaves fluttered her eyelashes.

'I must admit I was tempted! I have the most terrible sweet tooth. Always have had. When I was a kid, I was never without something in my mouth. I just *crave* it, night and day. So when I went to Dorothy's room with the others, later that evening, I was naughty. I blush to say so, but, well, to make a clean bosom of the thing, I stole a sip of Dorothy's cocoa. More like a gulp, actually.'

She smiled at Jarvis, who gazed expressionlessly back. Time had stopped. The crowd had fallen silent and the referee's breath, drawn to blow the final whistle, remained blockaded in his lungs. Only the ball was still moving, smooth and dreamlike, through the heavy air . . .

'Well, it's quite true that crime doesn't pay!' she went on jocularly. 'As soon as I tasted the cocoa, I realized that Miss Davis must have been teasing me. There *was* a lot of sugar in it, but it still tasted bitter. Really sharp, it was, with a sort of chemical edge to it. Funny, that.'

. . . hopelessly low and wide, but about to take that freakish deflection which would place it at the feet of the Accrington centre-forward . . .

'And it's no use you asking me about anything after that,' Mavis Hargreaves concluded with an embarrassed shrug, 'because I was fast asleep. I usually suffer from the most terrible insomnia, but that night I slept like the dead. The next thing I knew it was broad daylight, and everyone else had been up for hours!'

She put her hand to her mouth.

'Except for poor Dorothy, of course.'

. . . and the huge stadium exploded as the final whistle blew, ending the most extraordinary match which the hallowed turf of Wembley had ever seen. Fans of both teams wept openly and embraced each other, their rivalry forgotten in mutual wonderment at this demonstration that miracles could still happen and anything was possible . . .

'Thank you,' Jarvis told Mrs Hargreaves.

He turned to Anderson with a glazedly formal expression.

'If you'll excuse me for a moment, sir, I'll just have a word with HQ from the car,' he said. 'And then I'll need to speak to you and your sister.'

PART THREE

Rosemary dibbed the forefinger of her left hand into the soft soil several times and drew it out again, the fingernail clogged with dirt. She ripped the top off the small brightly coloured envelope she was holding in her other hand, and poured a stream of tiny black grains into her palm.

'You see?' she muttered fiercely. 'They come from Suttons at 75p a packet, you old fool!'

A car came down the tree-lined drive leading to the road which ran along the top of the ridge. It crunched across the weed-strewn gravel sweep in front of the house and drew up by the front door. Two men got out, looking about them.

Rosemary wiped the tears from her cheeks with her sleeve. Bending over the flowerbed, she busied herself with the seeds, letting each fall into its shallow grave and smoothing the earth over it.

'Afternoon.'

Detective Inspector Stanley Jarvis stood looking at Rosemary from the other side of the flowerbed. His companion, who wore dark glasses and appeared to be chewing gum, remained by the car.

'Good afternoon, Inspector,' Rosemary replied.

Jarvis nodded sagely.

'Planting something?' he observed.

'Just a few seeds.'

'Bit late for that, isn't it?'

Rosemary did not reply. Jarvis walked round the flowerbed and plucked the packet from her fingers.

'Poppies?' he exclaimed. 'I never knew they needed sowing. Thought they just happened.'

'They do grow wild, of course, but sometimes nature can do with a helping hand.'

Retrieving the packet, she filled the rest of the hollows with seeds.

'It's much the same as planting clues in a whodunnit, if you like,' she mused. 'It may seem a bit contrived, but the results are so much more interesting than the dreary crimes you read about in the papers.'

Jarvis made a face.

'I *don't* like,' he said. 'Now then, do you know where Mrs Hargreaves is? My colleague and I are here to take her statement.'

'I believe, in the house. Go through the French windows, I should. No one will mind, and it's quicker.'

Jarvis nodded briskly.

'Right you are. Tomkins!'

The two men converged on the house. Rosemary upended the packet of seeds, scattering the remainder across the flowerbed.

'There, now,' she murmured. 'You'll just have to fend for yourselves. I've interfered quite enough as it is.'

She raised one arm in response to a wave from Jack Weatherby, who had appeared from the grove of rhododendrons beyond the croquet lawn. He called out something that Rosemary couldn't quite catch.

'Yes, isn't it?' she returned heartily.

With a broad smile, Weatherby continued along the path. In his straw hat and linen suit, recovered from a trunk of his belongings discovered in the attic, he looked and moved like a younger brother of the man who used to sit slumped in his chair by the fireplace until the time came to shuffle back to bed. A change no less dramatic was to be seen in the other residents of Eventide Lodge. It was only now that Rosemary realized the extent to which she had come to accept that their condition was an inevitable consequence of the ageing process, only to be expected in people who were virtually at death's door. She had been astounded by the effect of a healthy diet, exercise, fresh air and renewed contact with their families and the outside world.

Not that the transition had been entirely smooth. Purvey was still under medical supervision after suffering a nervous collapse due to his belief that the 'new owners' were going to turn him out. Charles Symes, too, was in hospital, the media interest in the affair having pushed him to the front of the queue for his operation. Even Rosemary had suffered mild attacks of anxiety following the abrupt collapse of the system which had ruled their lives for so long. The day the plastic sheeting covering the windows had been torn down had been particularly fraught, with both Grace Lebon and Samuel Rossiter requiring sedation. But by far the worst affected had been Belinda Scott, who tried to get the others to join her in a campaign of passive resistance to the changes. When that failed, she had gone on hunger strike, accusing everyone else of betraying the rightful authority of Mr Anderson and

Miss Davis and threatening to exact a terrible retribution when they returned.

However, the chances of that happening were remote indeed. The charges of wilful cruelty and gross neglect on which the siblings had been arrested the previous week had been substantiated beyond a vestige of doubt both by the residents' statements and by the evidence of the medical examinations they had all undergone. The discovery that a resident of the Lodge named Hilary Bryant, who had since died, had been persuaded to alter her will in the Andersons' favour, and that pressure had been put on others to do the same, had sealed their fate. Even if by some miracle they escaped a prison sentence, their careers in residential care for the aged were quite clearly over.

Pending further developments, Eventide Lodge had been placed in the care of the Local Health Authority, who had staffed it with personnel recently been made redundant owing to the closure of the geriatric wing of a hospital in another part of the county. Their cheerful attentions had done wonders to awaken the residents from the catatonic stupor and paranoid delusions into which most of them had retreated, but an equally important factor had been the letters, phone calls and visits from friends and relatives horrified to learn what had been going on behind the genteel façade which the Andersons had maintained – and ashamed that they had not made it their business to find out earlier.

In the attic of the Lodge, the new staff had found over twenty dustbin liners crammed with post which the Andersons had deliberately withheld to increase the residents' sense of isolation and dependence. All outgoing letters were read by Anderson or Miss Davis, and any reference to conditions at the Lodge censored. The resulting anodyne communications served to persuade the recipients – not that they usually needed much persuasion – that their nominally beloved but in practice rather tiresome old relatives were as well as could be expected, and that phone calls and visits were pointlessly upsetting for everyone concerned. On the rare occasions when family members did insist on paying their respects in person, the residents were reduced to incoherent passivity by dosing their food with drugs prescribed by the compliant Dr Morel.

Rosemary made her way across the lawn to the garden seat which stood on the path at the foot of the rockery. She sat down and felt in her pocket for the letter she had received that morning. But it was another piece of paper that emerged, crumpled and soiled, with her name written on one side in shaky capitals. Hastily replacing it, Rosemary located the air-mail envelope with its large, colourful stamps in an unfamiliar currency.

She read the enclosure from beginning to end several times, then lay back on the slats of teak weathered to a silvery sheen, basking in the weak autumnal sunshine. A council employee was at work mowing the lawn at the other side of the house. Rosemary gazed up at the sky of hazy blue seamed with strata of diffuse cloud. The throaty purring of the motor-mower reminded her of the flimsy biplanes of her youth, when flying was still an adventure. She closed her eyes . . .

A shadow fell between her and the sun. Rosemary looked up to find Stanley Jarvis standing in front of her. His expression was unsympathetic.

'Have you been winding me up?' he said.

Rosemary peered at him, pondering the meaning of these words. She thought of the tin soldiers her brother had used to play with before a real war killed him, and was on the point of making a joke about clockwork toys when Jarvis went on.

'Mrs Hargreaves now refuses to confirm her earlier testimony about the cocoa.'

Rosemary brushed some grass clippings off her dress.

'How very tiresome of her,' she murmured.

'Don't give me that!' Jarvis snarled.

He fixed her with a stare.

'Perhaps you don't appreciate what's at stake here, Miss Travis. When I came here last week, Mrs Hargreaves told me that Miss Davis had specifically warned her against taking the blue mug of cocoa, claiming that it had extra sugar in it as a special treat for Mrs Davenport. Mrs Hargreaves went on to say that when she tasted the cocoa in Mrs Davenport's room later she found that it had a bitter taste with a, quote, sort of chemical edge to it, unquote, and that she slept exceptionally long and soundly that night.'

'I hope you'll forgive my saying so, Inspector, but . . . '

'The implications are quite clear. The cocoa intended for Mrs Davenport had in fact been dosed with crushed sleeping tablets, and since Miss Davis warned Mrs Hargreaves against taking it, she must have been a party to this. Everything else then falls into place. The morphine syrup was adulterated with blue curaçao, one of Miss Davis's favourite drinks. Once Mrs Davenport was unconscious, Purvey's missing syringe – which he saw Miss Davis take from his room – was used to inject the lethal dose of morphine. You discovered the body very early next morning and raised the alarm, and Mr Channing overheard the Andersons' panic as they struggled to set the scene of the supposed suicide before my officers arrived.'

'I feel that the real problem, Inspector, is that you . . . '

'But the credibility of that entire scenario depends on the crucial fact of Mrs Hargreaves's testimony, which she has now withdrawn! According to what she's just told me and Tomkins, she took her usual mug that evening. As for Mrs Davenport's cocoa, she has no idea what it may or may not have tasted like because she didn't try it, and she slept neither better nor worse than usual. In other words, the whole episode was fiction from beginning to end.'

Jarvis wagged his forefinger under Rosemary's nose.

'And *you* were the author! She told me that you put her up to it!'

Rosemary gave him a pitying look.

'You can't believe everything a suspect tells you, you know.'

'Mrs Hargreaves is not a bloody suspect!' Jarvis retorted.

Rosemary nodded earnestly.

'That is precisely the problem. As I've tried to point out to you on several occasions, your approach to this case has been flawed from the start. You arrived here convinced that Dorothy committed suicide, and it was only with the greatest difficulty that I was able to persuade you otherwise. You then abandoned that error only to rush headlong into another, and assume that the Andersons were the guilty parties. This blinkered approach not only prevented you from examining the case in the open-minded and impartial manner befitting a detective, but has also made it possible for the person really responsible to manipulate the situation to his – or her – advantage.'

Jarvis regarded her with mingled suspicion and curiosity.

'Meaning what?' he demanded.

'Has it really not occurred to you that there might be another explanation for Mrs Hargreaves telling you a story which she now admits was untrue?'

'You mean . . . ' groped Jarvis.

'I mean, my dear Inspector, that it was intended to divert suspicion from herself!'

Jarvis looked utterly baffled.

'But I *don't* suspect her! I've never suspected her for a single moment!'

Rosemary sighed.

'I believe you,' she said in a kindly tone. 'But to those who know you less well, like Mavis Hargreaves, such naïvety would have seemed almost impossible to credit from someone in your position. She would therefore have concluded that you were in fact playing a very deep game, pretending to suspect the Andersons in order to put the rest of us off our guard, and sought to cover her tracks by inventing the episode of Miss Davis and the cocoa, whose authorship she now attributes to me.'

She gave him a wry smile.

'And you must admit, Inspector, it worked a treat!'

Jarvis looked longingly at the police car. His colleague lay spread-eagled on the bonnet, soaking up the sunshine, his foot wagging in time to some inaudible music.

'How did you know Tomkins was from the island?' he asked.

'My mother was from the New Forest, but I was raised in Ryde,' Rosemary explained. 'The children at school used to call me a foreigner, because I was born on the mainland. I can still hear their mocking voices. The accent is unmistakable.'

'Ryde,' mused Jarvis.

He smiled. 'Remember the Beatles? Okay, I used to think, so she's got a ticket to Ryde. Why should that mean she doesn't care?'

'It's not just the islanders,' said Rosemary. 'People in general can be very heartless.'

Jarvis gazed into the distance, lost in thought.

'As for the beetles,' Rosemary went on, 'I certainly do remember them. But I'm glad to say that we're no longer troubled by them since the council fumigated the rooms.'

'That was when I first started to take you seriously,' Jarvis muttered almost inaudibly. 'If she's on to Tomkins, I thought, she can't be as far gone as this Anderson is trying to make out.'

He considered the grass at his feet for some time.

'Just the same,' he resumed, 'I don't think much of this Hargreaves angle. Apart from anything else, she doesn't have a motive.'

'I wouldn't be so sure, Inspector. Shortly before her death, Dorothy asked to see a solicitor with a view to changing her will. The Andersons believed that the alteration was in their favour, but I think that very unlikely. Hilary Bryant made the mistake of thinking that the prospect of the inheritance might soften the Andersons' hearts, but they were if anything even more beastly to her afterwards. With that example before her, I can't imagine that Dorothy would have allowed herself to be swayed, particularly since she knew it was likely she would have to go into hospital anyway. On the other hand, what more likely, under those circumstances, that she should have wished to settle her affairs, and that she should have decided that her close friend Mavis Hargreaves was a more suitable beneficiary than her apparently ungrateful and neglectful relatives?'

A dreamy smile spread across Jarvis's face.

'Of course!' he breathed. 'Why didn't I see it before? The solution's been staring me in the face all along!'

He looked keenly at Rosemary.

'We were quite excited about that aspect of the case for a few days there, but we rather lost interest when it transpired that Mrs Davenport had in fact instructed the solicitor to make over her estate to Miss Rosemary Travis.'

Rosemary sprang to her feet.

'No!' she broke out hoarsely. 'It's not true!'

Jarvis gave a smile of triumph.

'You've played a very clever game, Miss Travis, and you nearly got away with it. Yes, Mrs Hargreaves's tale about the cocoa was indeed intended to deceive us, but she didn't dream it up. Mavis Hargreaves isn't a detective story addict any more than she was Dorothy Davenport's close friend. You, on the other hand, are both!'

He thrust an accusing finger at her.

'Who had a better opportunity to poison the morphine syrup than the person who went to Mrs Davenport's room to fetch it just a few hours before her death?

The only fingerprints found on the bottle, apart from those of the deceased, were yours, Miss Travis! *Your* sleeping tablets were used to adulterate the cocoa, and you admit spending a considerable time alone with the victim after everyone else had left and the lights had been turned off. Your room is directly opposite that of Mr Purvey, whose door is always open. He assumed that the woman he saw taking his syringe was Miss Davis, because of the smell of alcohol, but it could equally well have been the person who had just entered Anderson's office and removed a quantity of blue curaçao!'

He stepped forward and gripped Rosemary's arm.

'I'm going to have to ask you to accompany me to headquarters, Miss Travis, and it's my duty to inform you that anything you say will be taken down and may be used in evidence against you.'

CHAPTER 12

'Don't be so ridiculous!' said Rosemary, snatching her arm free.

'What do you mean, ridiculous?' Jarvis retorted. 'You had the motive, the means and the opportunity. What more do you need?'

Rosemary snorted incredulously.

'Dorothy Davenport was my friend!' she exclaimed. 'I was closer to her than I've ever been to anyone in my life. I could no more have killed her than I could kill my own child.'

'Don't start dragging psychology into it!' snapped Jarvis. 'You told me all I needed to do was observe the rules, spot the clues and make the appropriate deductions. Well I've done that, Miss Travis, and they lead straight to you.'

Rosemary smiled mischievously.

'Ah, well as to that, you see, there's one clue I haven't told you about.'

She took a folded piece of paper from her pocket and handed it to him. Jarvis opened out the page. MISS ROSE-MARY TRAVIS was written in blue ballpoint on one side. He turned it over and read the lines of wavery writing on the other side.

Rose my dear,

This is not easy, particularly after everyone has been so kind. But it is the only way. They say laughter is what distinguishes us from the animals, but this does too, and just as clearly. They kill each other, but never themselves. Mr Darwin's law is their cage, but we're free to enjoy this last laugh at the universe's expense.

I can't think of freedom without thinking of all those I am leaving behind, and especially you, Rose. What will become of you without me to fuss over and care for? I dread the idea of you ending up like the others, yet that's what will happen if you stay here. You're strong, Rose, but in the end they will grind you down.

One possibility, if you are clever enough to take advantage of it, would be to make it look as though I were the victim in one of our whodunnits. The details I leave to you, dear Rose, who were always so much better at them than me, but I can at least provide the body. The investigation will reveal that death was due to an overdose of morphine syrup and some sleeping tablets which I took from your room. Just to be on the safe side, I also propose to drink the contents of those hideous miniatures which someone gave me for Christmas years and years ago and which I have always kept, for a reason which is only now clear to me.

Don't be afraid, Rose. I'm not.

Dot.

Jarvis folded the letter carefully.

'For all I know, this could be another of your tricks.'

'You can compare the handwriting with those letters of Dorothy's which were never posted,' Rosemary replied. 'But you need have no fear, Inspector. Having achieved the aims laid down by Dorothy in her letter, I have broken my staff and drowned my book.'

She slumped down on the garden seat again.

'Is it true about the will?'

'You mean to say she didn't tell you?' Jarvis demanded incredulously.

Rosemary shook her head.

'Of course not. Dorothy was much too considerate to have burdened the final days of our friendship with such an embarrassing revelation.'

Jarvis held up the letter.

'Assuming this *is* genuine,' he said heavily, 'I can do you for conspiracy to pervert.'

Rosemary gave a refined shrug.

'That's up to you, Inspector. Personally speaking, I wouldn't have thought that it would have made a very favourable impression. At all events, I take it that you are no longer proposing to "do" me for murder.'

Jarvis stared blankly at her for a moment, then abruptly burst out laughing.

'Don't tell me you fell for it!'

Rosemary flushed.

'I beg your pardon?'

Jarvis sat down on the seat and slapped Rosemary's knee familiarly.

'You really believed I was going to arrest you, didn't you?'

'I must admit you sounded awfully convincing,' she replied.

Jarvis nodded.

'So did you, Miss Travis, when you told me if I left without speaking to Mrs Hargreaves then you'd be the next to die. I didn't believe you really were in danger, of course, but just a moment there I thought that *you* did. Well, now I've got my own back!'

Rosemary looked him in the eye.

'I meant exactly what I said, Inspector.'

Jarvis waved Dorothy's letter in her face.

'You can't have it both ways! You now admit you knew all along that Mrs Davenport hadn't been murdered, so why on earth should you think you would be?'

Rosemary shook her head.

'You weren't paying attention, Inspector. You heard what you wanted to hear, not the actual words that were spoken. That's why people fail to guess the solution to detective stories, even though they've been given all the clues.'

'You told me you would be the next to die,' insisted Jarvis. 'Those were your very words.'

'And you assumed that by "die" I meant "be murdered".'

Jarvis narrowed his eyes.

'You mean . . . You meant . . . '

Rosemary nodded.

'If it had come to that, yes. I couldn't let Dorothy's sacrifice go for nothing.'

Jarvis looked at her.

'I believe you would, too.'

Rosemary smiled.

'But fortunately for both of us,' she said, 'it didn't come to that. Dot meant well, but she was always a bit vague when it came to working out the details of the plot. Left to my own devices, I'd have led you a merry old dance! As it was, of course, I had to improvise. There was no time to attempt anything really interesting.'

Jarvis got out his notebook.

'Right then, let's have it from the beginning.'

Rosemary groaned.

'Must we, Inspector? I must confess that my heart always sinks at the prospect of the scene where All Is Explained.'

'There has to be one, though, doesn't there?'

Rosemary nodded resignedly.

'Very well, I shall try and be as concise as possible.'

Jarvis licked his pencil.

'It was still early when I discovered Dorothy's body,' Rosemary began, 'but I knew it would not be long before people were up and about, so I had to work quickly. First I went downstairs to the study and added some of that blue liqueur to the remnants of the morphine syrup.'

'How did you know it was there?' prompted Jarvis.

'Miss Davis used to drink cocktails made with different-coloured liqueurs, including a blue one, arranged in layers. I don't know how she managed to stop them all getting mixed up . . .'

'Back of a spoon. One of Tomkins's party tricks. They should get together, that pair. Talk about a marriage made in hell.'

'I then washed out the miniature spirit bottles which Dorothy had drunk from and replaced them in their wooden case,' Rosemary went on.

'Why not just throw them away?'

'Someone might have noticed if the set had been

missing, but it was very unlikely that anyone would bother to check whether the bottles still had their original contents or not. After that I ground up some sleeping tablets and added the powder to the dregs of her cocoa. Finally, I crept into Mr Purvey's room, removed one of his syringes and left part of the plastic wrapping on the floor near the head of Dorothy's bed.'

Jarvis whistled quietly.

'With her still in it?'

'I was acting as Dorothy's executor, Inspector. She had given me my instructions. How could I not have carried them out to the best of my ability?'

'Go on,' said Jarvis above the sound of his scribbling pencil.

'At length Dorothy's absence was remarked and the alarm raised. My principal concern, of course, was to ensure that no one tampered with the items of evidence I had prepared. To that end I refused to leave Dorothy's room until the police arrived. Miss Davis tried to remove me, but I made such a fuss that in the end she gave up and left me there. I took advantage of this to stage a brief conversational exchange for the benefit of Mr Channing next door. My voice is deep enough to do a passable imitation of Anderson, particularly when muffled by the wall. My purpose in all this was to provide clues for your officers to collect when they arrived. In the event, however, they made no attempt to speak to any of the residents, let alone Channing, and even failed to notice the medicine and the cocoa by Dorothy's bed until I pointed them out.'

She turned round, pointing to the other policeman, who was now prancing about on the gravel yelling,

'Assume the position, motherfucker!' at his shadow on the car.

'Tell me, Inspector, why does your colleague try and conceal his myopia by wearing those ridiculous shaded glasses?'

Jarvis shook his head.

'Don't ask,' he sighed.

'I only mention the matter because it's so very dispiriting to have to bring the finer points of one's work to people's attention,' Rosemary went on. 'Even once I'd got him to notice the morphine bottle and the mug of cocoa, your colleague didn't seem capable of grasping their significance until I explained it to him. As for the wrapping from the syringe, I dropped a brooch right beside it and got him to pick it up for me to save my bad back and he *still* didn't see it. In the end I retrieved it myself and replaced it before you arrived. I knew that once the morphine and the cocoa had been analysed someone was bound to come to question me about the allegations I'd made. I just hoped it would be someone of a rather higher calibre – as happily proved to be the case.'

She smiled graciously at Jarvis.

'As soon as we met, Inspector, I sensed that you were someone who would respond to a challenge. I therefore proceeded by indirection, continually insisting that the murderer must be one of the residents and refusing to consider the Andersons as possible suspects, despite the evidence against them which I kept bringing to your notice. I also deliberately avoided any mention of the syringe, even though the prescribed dose of morphine clearly wouldn't have been enough to kill Dorothy. I thought you would enjoy thinking that you'd outwitted me there.'

Jarvis had stopped making notes. He opened his mouth to say something, then shook his head.

'Once you had gone upstairs to see Channing,' Rosemary continued, 'I had to find some way of distracting the Andersons' attentions while you spoke to the others. I took a chance and approached Mrs Hargreaves, who had been unexpectedly kind to me the day before. She gamely agreed to create a diversion by breaking out and hiding in the grounds. Miss Davis assaulted her violently when she found her, and warned her of even more brutal reprisals if she said anything to you, but despite her origins I'm glad to say that Mavis proved to be an absolute brick. She produced the story I had taught her about the cocoa, and luckily you believed her.'

Jarvis folded up his notebook and put it away in his pocket together with Dorothy's letter.

'I did what?' he inquired urbanely.

Rosemary eyed him.

'Well, you *did*, didn't you?'

Jarvis laughed.

'My dear Miss Travis, you surely don't think that a police officer of twenty years' experience can be deceived by such moonshine? This isn't one of your detective stories where some old lady runs rings round Inspector Clod. This is real life.'

Rosemary assumed a politely quizzical expression.

'But you arrested them, didn't you?'

'Yes, on charges of cruelty and neglect arising from what I'd learned about conditions here at the Lodge,' Jarvis returned.

'You didn't need to wait for Mavis's testimony to do that!'

'No, but once Anderson had overheard her trying to frame him and his sister, I *had* to act. What would have happened if I'd left her there? That pair would have beaten her within an inch of her life, wouldn't they?'

Rosemary nodded.

'But if you knew all along that the whole thing was a hoax, why did you get so fearfully cross when Mavis refused to confirm her earlier testimony just now? For that matter, why come at all?'

Jarvis smiled at her.

'I came to see you,' he said.

'Me?'

He nodded.

'I just dropped by to see how you were getting on.'

Rosemary looked flustered.

'But you seemed so angry!' she protested. 'All that business about feeling like a clockwork toy.'

Jarvis laughed.

'You're not the only one who can play a part, Miss Travis!'

Rosemary fixed him with a cool stare.

'Well, anyway, it comes to the same thing in the end.' She bit her lip.

'Do you think it *is* the end, Inspector?'

Jarvis rubbed his forehead.

'Well, I don't know. You've left me quite a little pile of loose ends to sort out, one way and another. But certainly you won't be seeing Anderson or his sister again, if that's what you mean.'

Rosemary shook her head minimally.

'I was thinking of Dorothy.'

'Sorry?'

Rosemary shook her head impatiently.

'Never mind. I was talking to myself, really.'

Jarvis blushed furiously.

'You mean do I believe in an afterlife?' he mumbled.

Rosemary said nothing.

'Well, I don't know,' he went on. 'I mean, I don't *not* believe in it.'

A faint smile appeared on Rosemary's lips.

'A good answer to a stupid question,' she said.

'How about you?' demanded Jarvis, seemingly stung by her condescending tone.

Rosemary considered, as though this was the first time the question had ever occurred to her.

'Well, I used not to.'

She paused.

'But now I'm not sure that I perhaps don't not believe in it any more.'

After a moment they looked at each other and both burst out laughing.

'What now?' asked Jarvis, standing up.

Rosemary consulted the watch she had been loaned by one of the nurses.

'It's nearly time for tea.'

'No, I meant generally. Are you going to stay here, or . . . ?'

She got to her feet, smiling broadly.

'Something really quite extraordinary has happened! Do you remember my nephew Stuart, the one I told you that you reminded me of when we first met? Well, just this morning I received a letter from him, completely out of the blue. It turns out that this affair has been on the news in Canada, and he's written asking if I'd like to go and stay with him and his wife for a while.'

Her smile faded.

'It might not work out, of course. We may not get on, or I may hate the place. But I must say I'm rather tempted.'

She glanced pertly at Jarvis.

'How's that for a happy ending?'

Jarvis grimaced.

'As you said earlier, Miss Travis, it seems a bit contrived.'

'If this were a story, perhaps. But as *you* said earlier, Inspector, this is real life, and life is perfectly shameless. It permits itself everything – even happiness.'

She looked down at the flowerbed and shivered.

'It's growing cold. Shall we go in?'